CU00841257

William Shakespeare's

Love's Labour's Lost
In Plain and Simple English

BookCaps Study Guides
www.bookcaps.com

© 2011. All Rights Reserved.

Table of Contents

About This Series

The "Classic Retold" series started as a way of telling classics for the modern reader—being careful to preserve the themes and integrity of the original. Whether you want to understand Shakespeare a little more or are trying to get a better grasps of the Greek classics, there is a book waiting for you!

The series is expanding every month. Visit BookCaps.com to see all the books in the series, and while you are there join the Facebook page, so you are first to know when a new book comes out.

Characters

FERDINAND, King of Navarre

BEROWNE, Lord attending on the King

LONGAVILLE, Lord attending on the King

DUMAINE, Lord attending on the King

BOYET, Lord attending on the Princess of France

MARCADE, Lord attending on the Princess of France

DON ADRIANO DE ARMADO, a fantastical Spaniard

SIR NATHANIEL, a Curate

HOLOFERNES, a Schoolmaster

DULL, a Constable

COSTARD, a Clown

MOTH, Page to Armado

A FORESTER

THE PRINCESS OF FRANCE

ROSALINE, Lady attending on the Princess

MARIA, Lady attending on the Princess

KATHARINE, Lady attending on the Princess

JAQUENETTA, a country wench

Officers and Others, Attendants on the King and Princess.

Play

ACT I

SCENE I. The king of Navarre's park.

Enter FERDINAND king of Navarre, BIRON, LONGAVILLE and DUMAIN

FERDINAND

Let fame, that all hunt after in their lives,
Live register'd upon our brazen tombs
And then grace us in the disgrace of death;
When, spite of cormorant devouring Time,
The endeavor of this present breath may buy
That honour which shall bate his scythe's keen edge
And make us heirs of all eternity.
Therefore, brave conquerors,--for so you are,
That war against your own affections
And the huge army of the world's desires,--
Our late edict shall strongly stand in force:
Navarre shall be the wonder of the world;
Our court shall be a little Academe,
Still and contemplative in living art.
You three, Biron, Dumain, and Longaville,
Have sworn for three years' term to live with me
My fellow-scholars, and to keep those statutes
That are recorded in this schedule here:
Your oaths are pass'd; and now subscribe your names,
That his own hand may strike his honour down
That violates the smallest branch herein:
If you are arm'd to do as sworn to do,
Subscribe to your deep oaths, and keep it too.

Let fame, which everyone seeks in their lives,
Live carved upon our brass tombs
And then honor us in the dishonor of death;
When, in spite of ravenous devouring Time,
The hard work of our lives may buy
That honor which blunts death's sharp blade
And make us all live forever.
And so, brave conquerors, --for that's what you are,
That war against your own feelings
And the huge army that is the world's desires
Our most recent law will strongly uphold:
Navarre will be the wonder of the world;
Our court will be like an academy,
Constant and thoughtful in living art.
You three Biron, Dumain, and Longaville,
Have sworn that you will live with me for three
year. My scholar-men, and to uphold the laws
That are recorded in this schedule here:
You have said your oaths, and now write your names,
So that his signature will be his downfall for
Whoever violates the smallest part of the oath
from here on out: If you are ready to do what
you've sworn to do, Sign here to affirm your
oaths, and keep them.

LONGAVILLE

I am resolved; 'tis but a three years' fast:
The mind shall banquet, though the body pine:
Fat paunches have lean pates, and dainty bits
Make rich the ribs, but bankrupt quite the wits.

I am determined; it will be like a fast for only
three years: The mind will banquet, though the
body will yearn: Fat stomachs have thin heads,
and delicate bits Make your ribs rich and
completely bankrupt your wits.

DUMAIN

My loving lord, Dumain is mortified:
The grosser manner of these world's delights
He throws upon the gross world's baser slaves:
To love, to wealth, to pomp, I pine and die;
With all these living in philosophy.

My gracious lord, Dumain is humiliated:
The abundance of these world's delights
He throws to this big world's lesser people:
To love, to wealth, to splendor, I yearn and die;
All of these things will only be thoughts to me.

BIRON
I can but say their protestation over;
So much, dear liege, I have already sworn,
That is, to live and study here three years.
But there are other strict observances;
As, not to see a woman in that term,
Which I hope well is not enrolled there;
And one day in a week to touch no food
And but one meal on every day beside,
The which I hope is not enrolled there;
And then, to sleep but three hours in the night,
And not be seen to wink of all the day—
When I was wont to think no harm all night
And make a dark night too of half the day—
Which I hope well is not enrolled there:
O, these are barren tasks, too hard to keep,
Not to see ladies, study, fast, not sleep!

FERDINAND
Your oath is pass'd to pass away from these.

BIRON
Let me say no, my liege, an if you please:
I only swore to study with your grace
And stay here in your court for three years'
space.

LONGAVILLE
You swore to that, Biron, and to the rest.

BIRON
By yea and nay, sir, then I swore in jest.
What is the end of study? let me know.

FERDINAND
Why, that to know, which else we should not
know.

BIRON
Things hid and barr'd, you mean, from common
sense?

FERDINAND
Ay, that is study's godlike recompense.

BIRON

I can only repeat what they have said;
I have already sworn so much, my dear liege,
Which is to live and study here for three years
But there are other strict rules;
Like, not being able to see a woman during that
time, Which I really hope is not required there;
And for one day a week not to touch any food
And only one meal on every day besides that,
Which I also hope is not required there;
And another, to only sleep three hours a night
And not being able to close your eyes all day—
When I have been used to sleeping all night
And also into half of the day—
Which I really hope is not required there
O, these are empty tasks, too hard to keep,
To not see any ladies, study, not eat, not sleep!

You've sworn an oath to give up these things.

Let me say no, my liege, if you'll permit me to
say: I only swore to study with your grace
And stay here in your court for three years'
time.

You did swear to that, Biron, and to everything
else.

Earnestly, sir, then I swore as a joke
What is the purpose of the study? Tell me.

Well, so that we can know things we wouldn't
know otherwise.

You mean things that are hidden and barred
from common sense?

Yes, that is the godlike reward of the study.

Come on, then; I will swear to study so,
To know the thing I am forbid to know:
As thus,--to study where I well may dine,
When I to feast expressly am forbid;
Or study where to meet some mistress fine,
When mistresses from common sense are hid;
Or, having sworn too hard a keeping oath,
Study to break it and not break my troth.
If study's gain be thus and this be so,
Study knows that which yet it doth not know:
Swear me to this, and I will ne'er say no.

FERDINAND
These be the stops that hinder study quite
And train our intellects to vain delight.

BIRON
Why, all delights are vain; but that most vain,
Which with pain purchased doth inherit pain:
As, painfully to pore upon a book
To seek the light of truth; while truth the while
Doth falsely blind the eyesight of his look:
Light seeking light doth light of light beguile:
So, ere you find where light in darkness lies,
Your light grows dark by losing of your eyes.
Study me how to please the eye indeed
By fixing it upon a fairer eye,
Who dazzling so, that eye shall be his heed
And give him light that it was blinded by.
Study is like the heaven's glorious sun
That will not be deep-search'd with saucy looks:
Small have continual plodders ever won
Save base authority from others' books
These earthly godfathers of heaven's lights
That give a name to every fixed star
Have no more profit of their shining nights
Than those that walk and wot not what they are.
Too much to know is to know nought but fame;
And every godfather can give a name.

FERDINAND
How well he's read, to reason against reading!

DUMAIN
Proceeded well, to stop all good proceeding!

Alright, then; I will swear to study this way,
So that I can know the thing I am forbidden to
know; So that, --I can learn where I can dine,
When I am expressly forbid to eat;
Or learn where to meet a fine lady,
When ladies are hidden from common sense;
Or, if I've sworn to keep an oath that's too hard
to keep, Learn how to break it and not break my
loyalty to the pledge. If that is what I will gain
by studying, Study knows the things that it
doesn't know yet: Swear me to this and I will
never say no.

These are the obstacles that greatly impede
studying And allure our intellects to selfish
delights.

Well all delights are selfish; but the most selfish,
Which as it is acquired with hard labor, it
inherits pain: Like, poring laboriously over a
book To seek the light of truth; and all the while
truth Treacherously blinds his eyesight and his
power to see: Searching for truth by excessive
study takes your eyes' ability to see,: Like, when
you stare at a bright light, It eventually blinds
you. Teach me how to please the eye indeed
By looking at the eyes of a beautiful woman,
That dazzles so much that it will be his safety
And it will give him the light that his eye was
blinded by. Study is like the heaven's glorious
sun That will not be scrutinized by insolent
looks: People who trudge on continuously win
very little Except for the lowest power from
others' books These earthly guardians of
heaven's lights That namde every immovable
star Get no more benefit from their starlit nights
Than those that walk around not knowing what
stars are. To know too much is to know nothing
but secondhand information; And every child's
godfather can give a name.

How well informed he is, to argue against
learning!

He is very advanced, to stop all advancement!

LONGAVILLE
He weeds the corn and still lets grow the weeding.

He pulls out the wheat and allows weeds to grow.

BIRON
The spring is near when green geese are a-breeding.

We know that spring is coming when the geese start breeding.

DUMAIN
How follows that?

What does that have to do with anything?

BIRON
Fit in his place and time.

Exactly in its place and time.

DUMAIN
In reason nothing.

It makes no sense.

BIRON
Something then in rhyme.

Maybe if I made it rhyme.

FERDINAND
Biron is like an envious sneaping frost,
That bites the first-born infants of the spring.

Biron is like a malicious nipping frost,
That kills the first-born buds of the spring.

BIRON
Well, say I am; why should proud summer boast
Before the birds have any cause to sing?
Why should I joy in any abortive birth?
At Christmas I no more desire a rose
Than wish a snow in May's new-fangled mirth;
But like of each thing that in season grows.
So you, to study now it is too late,
Climb o'er the house to unlock the little gate.

Well, say I am; why should glorious summer boast Before the birds have any cause to sing? Why should I take joy in a failed birth? At Christmas I don't wish that roses would grow Any more than I wish for snow to ruin the new joy of spring in May; But each things grows in its own season. Just like you, to study now is too late, Climb over the house and unlock the little gate.

FERDINAND
Well, sit you out: go home, Biron: adieu.

Well, you sit out: go home Biron; goodbye.

BIRON
No, my good lord; I have sworn to stay with you:
And though I have for barbarism spoke more
Than for that angel knowledge you can say,
Yet confident I'll keep what I have swore
And bide the penance of each three years' day.
Give me the paper; let me read the same;
And to the strict'st decrees I'll write my name.

No, my good lord; I have sworn to stay with you: And though I have been speaking more for the uncultured Than for the angel that is knowledge, Yet I'm confident that I will keep my oaths And stay for the three years of penance. Give me the paper; let me read the oaths; And sign myself to the strictest rules.

FERDINAND
How well this yielding rescues thee from shame!

How well you've rescued yourself from shame by giving in!

BIRON
[Reads] 'Item, That no woman shall come within a
mile of my court:' Hath this been proclaimed?

'Note, That no woman will come within a mile of my court:' Has this been proclaimed?

LONGAVILLE
Four days ago.

Four days ago.

BIRON
Let's see the penalty.

Let's see what the penalty is.

Reads

'On pain of losing her tongue.' Who devised this penalty?

'If caught, she will lose her tongue.' Who came up with this penalty?

LONGAVILLE
Marry, that did I.

That was me.

BIRON
Sweet lord, and why?

Why, sweet lord?

LONGAVILLE
To fright them hence with that dread penalty.

To frighten them away form such a horrible penalty.

BIRON
A dangerous law against gentility!

A dangerous law against nobility!

Reads

'Item, If any man be seen to talk with a woman
within the term of three years, he shall endure such
public shame as the rest of the court can
possibly devise.'
This article, my liege, yourself must break;
For well you know here comes in embassy
The French king's daughter with yourself to speak—
A maid of grace and complete majesty—
About surrender up of Aquitaine

*'Note, If any man be seen to talk with a woman within the term of three years, he will suffer whatever
public shame that the rest of the court can possibly come up with.'
This rule, my liege, you yourself are going to have to break; You know very well that on their way in embassy Is the The French king's daughter, to speak with you--
A graceful and majestic woman--
About the surrender of Aquitaine*

To her decrepit, sick and bedrid father:
Therefore this article is made in vain,
Or vainly comes the admired princess hither.

FERDINAND
What say you, lords? Why, this was quite forgot.

BIRON
So study evermore is overshot:
While it doth study to have what it would
It doth forget to do the thing it should,
And when it hath the thing it hunteth most,
'Tis won as towns with fire, so won, so lost.

FERDINAND
We must of force dispense with this decree;
She must lie here on mere necessity.

BIRON
Necessity will make us all forsworn
Three thousand times within this three years' space;
For every man with his affects is born,
Not by might master'd but by special grace:
If I break faith, this word shall speak for me;
I am forsworn on 'mere necessity.'
So to the laws at large I write my name:
Subscribes
And he that breaks them in the least degree
Stands in attainder of eternal shame:
Suggestions are to other as to me;
But I believe, although I seem so loath,
I am the last that will last keep his oath.
But is there no quick recreation granted?

FERDINAND
Ay, that there is. Our court, you know, is haunted
With a refined traveller of Spain;
A man in all the world's new fashion planted,
That hath a mint of phrases in his brain;
One whom the music of his own vain tongue
Doth ravish like enchanting harmony;
A man of complements, whom right and wrong
Have chose as umpire of their mutiny:

To her sick, dying, bedridden father:
Therefore this rule is useless,
Or it's useless for the beautiful princess to come here.

What do you say lords? We seem to have completely forgotten this.

And so study is always overshot:
While it studies to learn what it can
It forgets to do what it's supposed to,
And what it has the thing it seeks the most,
It's won like towns with fire, won and then lost.

We are going to have to do away with this decree; She comes here for a necessity.

Necessity will make us all break our vows
Three thousand times within these three years;
For every man is born with feelings,
That are not mastered by strength, but by a special grace:
If I break my vows, this word will defend me;
I broke them because of 'necessity'
So with the laws at large, I write my name:
Signs
And whoever breaks them in the smallest degree
Will be disgraced by eternal shame:
Suggestions are to others as well as me;
But I think, although I seem so reluctant,
That I will be the last man to keep his oath.
But will permission not be granted for some quick enjoyment before we start?

Yes, there will be. Our court, you know, is haunted
By an elegant traveler from Spain;
A man who is very knowledgeable of the world,
That has a store of phrases in his brain;
Whose musical native language
Enraptures like an enchanting harmony;
A man who gives out compliments, whom right and wrong Have chosen to be the judge of their

This child of fancy, that Armado hight,
For interim to our studies shall relate
In high-born words the worth of many a knight
From tawny Spain lost in the world's debate.
How you delight, my lords, I know not, I;
But, I protest, I love to hear him lie
And I will use him for my minstrelsy.

mutiny: This child of fancy called Armado,
In the meantime during our studies will tell us
In eloquent words the worth of many a knight
From tan-colored Spain that were killed in the
world's wars. I don't know how much he will
delight you; But I must say that I love to hear
him lie And I will use him for my troupe of
entertainers.

BIRON
Armado is a most illustrious wight,
A man of fire-new words, fashion's own knight.

Armado is a very famous creature,
A man with new words like fire, a knight of
making shapes and forms.

LONGAVILLE
Costard the swain and he shall be our sport;
And so to study, three years is but short.

The young man Costard and he will entertain
us; And so let's get to studying, three years is a
short time.

Enter DULL with a letter, and COSTARD

DULL
Which is the duke's own person?

Which one of you is the duke's person?

BIRON
This, fellow: what wouldst?

That's me: what do you want?

DULL
I myself reprehend his own person, for I am his
grace's tharborough: but I would see his own
person
in flesh and blood.

I myself am above his person, since I am
The King's officer: but I must see the duke
himself,
His own flesh and blood.

BIRON
This is he.

I am the duke.

DULL
Signior Arme--Arme--commends you. There's
villany
abroad: this letter will tell you more.

Mister Arme—Arme—writes to you. There's foul
work
abroad: this letter will tell you more.

COSTARD
Sir, the contempts thereof are as touching me.

Sir, the contemptuous things it mentions are
regarding me.

FERDINAND
A letter from the magnificent Armado.

A letter from the magnificent Armado.

BIRON

How low soever the matter, I hope in God for
high words.

*However bad the matter is, I hope to God for
good words.*

LONGAVILLE
A high hope for a low heaven: God grant us
patience!

*A high hope for a low heaven: God grant us
patience!*

BIRON
To hear? or forbear laughing?

To hear the letter? or to keep from laughing?

LONGAVILLE
To hear meekly, sir, and to laugh moderately; or
to
forbear both.

*To hear submissively, sir, and to laugh in
moderation; or to
Do neither.*

BIRON
Well, sir, be it as the style shall give us cause to
climb in the merriness.

*Well, sir, hopefully the manner of it will give us
cause to Be more cheerful.*

COSTARD
The matter is to me, sir, as concerning
Jaquenetta.
The manner of it is, I was taken with the
manner.

*The matter is about me sir, concerning
Jaquenetta,
The manner of it is that I was taken with the
manner.*

BIRON
In what manner?

In what manner?

COSTARD
In manner and form following, sir; all those
three:
I was seen with her in the manor-house, sitting
with
her upon the form, and taken following her into
the
park; which, put together, is in manner and form
following. Now, sir, for the manner,--it is the
manner of a man to speak to a woman: for the
form,--
in some form.

*In manner and form following, sir; all those
three:
I was seen with her in the manor-house, sitting
with
Her on the frame, and taken when I was
following her into the
park; which put together is in the manner and
form following. Now, sir, for the manner,-- it is
the nature of a man to speak to a woman: now
for the form,--
In some form.*

BIRON
For the following, sir?

And what about the following?

COSTARD
As it shall follow in my correction: and God

It will follow that I will be corrected: and God

defend
the right!

defend
The right!

FERDINAND
Will you hear this letter with attention?

Will you hear this letter with consideration?

BIRON
As we would hear an oracle.

Like we would hear an oracle.

BIRON
As we would hear an oracle.

Like we would hear an oracle.

COSTARD
Such is the simplicity of man to hearken after
the flesh.

Such is the simplicity of a man following his
desires of the flesh.

FERDINAND
[Reads] 'Great deputy, the welkin's vicegerent
and
sole dominator of Navarre, my soul's earth's
god,
and body's fostering patron.'

[Reads] 'Great deputy, Heaven's agent and
sole dominator of Navarre, the god of my soul's
earth,
And the one who guards and fosters my body.'

COSTARD
Not a word of Costard yet.

He hasn't even mentioned me yet.

FERDINAND
[Reads] 'So it is,'—

[Reads] 'So it is,'—

COSTARD
It may be so: but if he say it is so, he is, in
telling true, but so.

It may be so: but if he says it's so, then he is,
Truly, only so.

FERDINAND
Peace!

Peace!

COSTARD
Be to me and every man that dares not fight!

Peace to me and every man that doesn't dare
fight!

FERDINAND
No words!

I mean no more words!

COSTARD
Of other men's secrets, I beseech you.

Yes, no more words of other men's secrets, I beg
you.

FERDINAND
[Reads] 'So it is, besieged with sable-coloured melancholy, I did commend the black-oppressing humour
to the most wholesome physic of thy health-giving
air; and, as I am a gentleman, betook myself to walk. The time when. About the sixth hour; when
beasts most graze, birds best peck, and men sit down
to that nourishment which is called supper: so much
for the time when. Now for the ground which; which,
I mean, I walked upon: it is y-cleped thy park. Then
for the place where; where, I mean, I did encounter
that obscene and preposterous event, that draweth
from my snow-white pen the ebon-coloured ink, which
here thou viewest, beholdest, surveyest, or seest; but to the place where; it standeth north-north-east
and by east from the west corner of thy curious-knotted garden: there did I see that low-spirited swain, that base minnow of thy mirth,'—

COSTARD
Me?

FERDINAND
[Reads] 'that unlettered small-knowing soul,'—

COSTARD
Me?

FERDINAND
[Reads] 'that shallow vassal,'—

COSTARD
Still me?

FERDINAND

[Reads] 'So it is, taken with a dark colored melancholy, I tried to get rid of the depressing mood
by going to the wholesome doctor that is the health-giving
air; and since I'm a gentleman, to myself on a walk. The time went by. At about six; when
the animals graze the most, birds peck the most, and men sit down
to have that nourishment which is called supper: so much
had time gone by. Now for which ground; which,
I mean, I had walked upon: it is called your park. Then
for the where; where, I mean, I encountered that indecent and ridiculous event, that draws from my snowy white pen the black colored ink, which
you view, behold, survey, or see here; but to the place where; it is north-north-east and by east from the west corner of your strange knotted garden: that's where I saw that mean-spirited
youth, that base minnow that amuses you,'--

Me?

[Reads] 'that uneducated, unwitting soul,'--

Me?

[Reads] 'that slow-minded subordinate,'—

Still me?

[Reads] 'which, as I remember, hight Costard,'—
O, me!

[Reads] 'which, as I remember, is named Costard,'-- Oh, me!

FERDINAND

[**Reads**] 'sorted and consorted, contrary to thy established proclaimed edict and continent canon,
which with,--O, with--but with this I passion to say
wherewith,--

*[Reads] 'planned and schemed, contrary to your established proclaimed edict and law
Which with, -- Oh, with—but with this I long to say
whereby,--*

COSTARD

With a wench.

With a girl.

FERDINAND

[Reads] 'with a child of our grandmother Eve, a female; or, for thy more sweet understanding, a woman. Him I, as my ever-esteemed duty pricks me on,
have sent to thee, to receive the meed of punishment, by thy sweet grace's officer, Anthony
Dull; a man of good repute, carriage, bearing, and
estimation.'

*[Reads] 'with a child of our grandmother Eve, a female; or, to make is easier for you to understand, a woman. I have, as my much respected duty commands me,
sent him to you, to receive the fitting reward of punishment by your sweet grace's officer, Anthony
Dull; a man with a good reputation, demeanor, behavior, and
respect.'*

DULL

'Me, an't shall please you; I am Anthony Dull.

It may please you to know; I am Anthony Dull.

FERDINAND

[Reads] 'For Jaquenetta,--so is the weaker vessel called which I apprehended with the aforesaid swain,--I keep her as a vessel of the law's fury; and shall, at the least of thy sweet notice, bring her to trial. Thine, in all compliments of devoted and heart-burning heat of duty.

[Reads] 'Since Jaquenetta, --that's what the weaker one is called that I apprehended with the afore mentioned young man, -- I keep her as a receptacle of the law's fury; and will, at your smallest command, bring her to trial. Yours truly, in all regards of devoted and heart-burning heat of duty.

DON ADRIANO DE ARMADO.'

BIRON

This is not so well as I looked for, but the best that ever I heard.

This is not as good as what I hoped for, but it's the best that I ever heard.

FERDINAND

Ay, the best for the worst. But, sirrah, what say

Yes, the best for the worst. But, slave, what do

you to this?

COSTARD
Sir, I confess the wench.

FERDINAND
Did you hear the proclamation?

COSTARD
I do confess much of the hearing it but little of the marking of it.

FERDINAND
It was proclaimed a year's imprisonment, to be taken
with a wench.

COSTARD
I was taken with none, sir: I was taken with a damsel.

FERDINAND
Well, it was proclaimed 'damsel.'

COSTARD
This was no damsel, neither, sir; she was a virgin.

FERDINAND
It is so varied, too; for it was proclaimed 'virgin.'

COSTARD
If it were, I deny her virginity: I was taken with a maid.

FERDINAND
This maid will not serve your turn, sir.

COSTARD
This maid will serve my turn, sir.

FERDINAND
Sir, I will pronounce your sentence: you shall fast
a week with bran and water.

you say to this?

Sir, I confess that I know the girl.

Did you hear the proclamation?

I confess to the hearing of it, but very little to paying attention to it.

*It was proclaimed that you will be imprisoned for a year if you are taken
with a girl.*

I wasn't taken with a girl: I was taken with a damsel.

Well, it was proclaimed that a 'damsel' counts too.

This wasn't a damsel either, sir; she was a virgin.

It is also varied to include 'virgins.'

If that's so then I deny her virginity and say: I was taken with a maid.

That won't help to serve your purpose either.

This maid will serve me, sir.

*Sir, I will give you your sentence: you will fast
For a week with bread and water only.*

COSTARD

I had rather pray a month with mutton and porridge.

I would rather pray for a month and be able to eat mutton and porridge.

FERDINAND

And Don Armado shall be your keeper.
My Lord Biron, see him deliver'd o'er:
And go we, lords, to put in practise that
Which each to other hath so strongly sworn.

*And Don Armado will keep watch over you.
My Lord Biron, see that he is delivered over there: And we will go, Lords, to put into practice that Which we have so strongly promised to each other.*

Exeunt FERDINAND, LONGAVILLE, and DUMAIN

BIRON

I'll lay my head to any good man's hat,
These oaths and laws will prove an idle scorn.
Sirrah, come on.

I'll bet my head to any good man's hat That these oaths and laws will prove to be a useless mockery. Slave, come on.

COSTARD

I suffer for the truth, sir; for true it is, I was taken with Jaquenetta, and Jaquenetta is a true girl; and therefore welcome the sour cup of prosperity! Affliction may one day smile again; and
till then, sit thee down, sorrow!

I suffer for the truth, sir; for it's true, I was Taken with Jaquenetta, and Jaquenetta is a true girl; and so we welcome the bitter taste of success! Sickness may one day smile again; and till then, I welcome you, sorrow!

Exeunt

SCENE II. The same.

Enter DON ADRIANO DE ARMADO and MOTH

DON ADRIANO DE ARMADO
Boy, what sign is it when a man of great spirit
grows melancholy?

Boy, what does it mean when a man who is usually energetic grows melancholy?

MOTH
A great sign, sir, that he will look sad.

It means, sir, that he will look sad.

DON ADRIANO DE ARMADO
Why, sadness is one and the self-same thing,
dear imp.

But sadness and melancholy are the same thing, dear dwarf.

MOTH
No, no; O Lord, sir, no.

No, no; O Lord, sir, I disagree.

DON ADRIANO DE ARMADO
How canst thou part sadness and melancholy,
my
tender juvenal?

What's the difference between them, my tender young man?

MOTH
By a familiar demonstration of the working, my
tough senior.

By a known demonstration of how it works, my tough elder.

DON ADRIANO DE ARMADO
Why tough senior? why tough senior?

Why tough elder? why tough elder?

MOTH
Why tender juvenal? why tender juvenal?

Why tender young man? why tender young man?

DON ADRIANO DE ARMADO
I spoke it, tender juvenal, as a congruent
epitheton
appertaining to thy young days, which we may
nominate tender.

I said it, tender young man, as an accurate description
Having to do with your young days, which we can accurately call tender.

MOTH
And I, tough senior, as an appertinent title to
your
old time, which we may name tough.

Me too, tough elder, as an appropriate title to your
old age, which we can call tough.

DON ADRIANO DE ARMADO

Pretty and apt.

Pretty and apt.

MOTH
How mean you, sir? I pretty, and my saying apt?
or

What do you mean, sir? I'm pretty and my words are apt?

I apt, and my saying pretty?

Or am I apt and my words pretty?

DON ADRIANO DE ARMADO
Thou pretty, because little.

You pretty, because you are little.

MOTH
Little pretty, because little. Wherefore apt?

Hardly pretty, because I'm little. And what is apt?

DON ADRIANO DE ARMADO
And therefore apt, because quick.

So you are apt, because you are quick.

MOTH
Speak you this in my praise, master?

Are you saying this as a compliment, master?

DON ADRIANO DE ARMADO
In thy condign praise.

It's a much deserved compliment.

MOTH
I will praise an eel with the same praise.

I will compliment an eel in the same way.

DON ADRIANO DE ARMADO
What, that an eel is ingenious?

What, that an eel is clever?

MOTH
That an eel is quick.

That an eel is quick.

DON ADRIANO DE ARMADO
I do say thou art quick in answers: thou heatest my blood.

I do say, you are quick in answers: you make me angry.

MOTH
I am answered, sir.

You are right, sir.

DON ADRIANO DE ARMADO
I love not to be crossed.

I do not like being crossed.

MOTH
[Aside] He speaks the mere contrary; crosses love not him.

[Aside] He's saying it backwards; crosses don't like him.

DON ADRIANO DE ARMADO
I have promised to study three years with the duke.

I have promised to study for three years with the duke.

MOTH
You may do it in an hour, sir.

You could do that in an hour, sir.

DON ADRIANO DE ARMADO
Impossible.

Impossible.

MOTH
How many is one thrice told?

How much is one times three?

DON ADRIANO DE ARMADO
I am ill at reckoning; it fitteth the spirit of a tapster.

I am bad at math; it suits a tavern keeper better.

MOTH
You are a gentleman and a gamester, sir.

You are a gentleman and a gambler, sir.

DON ADRIANO DE ARMADO
I confess both: they are both the varnish of a complete man.

I confess to both: they are both the sign of a Complete man.

MOTH
Then, I am sure, you know how much the gross sum of
deuce-ace amounts to.

Then, I am sure, you know how much the sum of A two and an ace amounts to.

DON ADRIANO DE ARMADO
It doth amount to one more than two.

It amounts to one more than two.

MOTH
Which the base vulgar do call three.

Which the lowly and vulgar call three.

DON ADRIANO DE ARMADO
True.

True.

MOTH
Why, sir, is this such a piece of study? Now here is three studied, ere ye'll thrice wink: and how easy it is to put 'years' to the word 'three,' and study three years in two words, the dancing horse
will tell you.

Why, sir, would you study for so long? Just now Three has been studied, before you've blinked three times: and how Easy it is to put 'years' next to the word 'three,' and Study three years in just two words, the dancing horse Will tell you.

DON ADRIANO DE ARMADO

A most fine figure!

What a fine way of figuring!

MOTH

To prove you a cipher.

To prove you are being cryptic.

DON ADRIANO DE ARMADO

I will hereupon confess I am in love: and as it is
base for a soldier to love, so am I in love with a
base wench. If drawing my sword against the
humour
of affection would deliver me from the
reprobate
thought of it, I would take Desire prisoner, and
ransom him to any French courtier for a new-
devised
courtesy. I think scorn to sigh: methinks I
should
outswear Cupid. Comfort, me, boy: what great
men
have been in love?

I will confess, I am in love: and as it is
Lowly for a soldier to love, so am I in love with
a Lowly girl. If drawing my sword against this
mood
Of affection would deliver from the immoral
Thought of it, I would make Desire my prisoner,
and
Ransom him to any French flatterer for some
new
Compliments. I despise sighing: I think I could
Outswear Cupid. Comfort me, boy: tell me what
great men
Have been in love?

MOTH

Hercules, master.

Hercules, master.

DON ADRIANO DE ARMADO

Most sweet Hercules! More authority, dear boy,
name
more; and, sweet my child, let them be men of
good
repute and carriage.

Yes, good Hercules! More powerful, dear boy,
name
More; and please, my child, make sure they are
men with good
Reputations and behavior.

MOTH

Samson, master: he was a man of good carriage,
great
carriage, for he carried the town-gates on his
back
like a porter: and he was in love.

Samson, master: he was a man of good deeds,
great
Deeds, he carried the town gates on his back
Like a doorman: and he was in love

DON ADRIANO DE ARMADO

O well-knit Samson! strong-jointed Samson! I
do
excel thee in my rapier as much as thou didst me
in
carrying gates. I am in love too. Who was

Oh, well-made Samson! Strong and mighty
Samson! I would
Beat you by sword as much as you would beat
me in
Carrying gates. I am in love too. Who was

Samson's
love, my dear Moth?

Samson's
Love, my dear Moth?

MOTH
A woman, master.

A woman, master.

DON ADRIANO DE ARMADO
Of what complexion?

What kind of character was she?

MOTH
Of all the four, or the three, or the two, or one of
the four.

She was all four, or three, or two, or one of the
four.

DON ADRIANO DE ARMADO
Tell me precisely of what complexion.

Tell me precisely what her character was like.

MOTH
Of the sea-water green, sir.

Of sea-water green, sir.

DON ADRIANO DE ARMADO
Is that one of the four complexions?

Is that one of the four characteristics of people?

MOTH
As I have read, sir; and the best of them too.

That's what I have read, sir; and the best of
them too.

DON ADRIANO DE ARMADO
Green indeed is the colour of lovers; but to have
a
love of that colour, methinks Samson had small
reason
for it. He surely affected her for her wit.

Green is indeed the color of lovers; but to have
a
Love of with that kind of color, I don't think
Samson had much reason
To love her for it. He surely was affectionate to
her for her cleverness.

MOTH
It was so, sir; for she had a green wit.

That's right, sir; she had a green wit.

DON ADRIANO DE ARMADO
My love is most immaculate white and red.

My love is the most flawless white and red.

MOTH
Most maculate thoughts, master, are masked
under
such colours.

Most unclean thoughts, master are masked and
hidden
By those colors.

DON ADRIANO DE ARMADO
Define, define, well-educated infant.

Tell me what you mean by that, you well-
educated infant.

MOTH
My father's wit and my mother's tongue, assist me!

My father's wit and my mother's words help me!

DON ADRIANO DE ARMADO
Sweet invocation of a child; most pretty and pathetical!

The sweet supplication of a child; very pretty and Pathetic!

MOTH
If she be made of white and red,
Her faults will ne'er be known,
For blushing cheeks by faults are bred
And fears by pale white shown:
Then if she fear, or be to blame,
By this you shall not know,
For still her cheeks possess the same
Which native she doth owe.
A dangerous rhyme, master, against the reason of
white and red.

If she is made of white and red,
Her faults will never be known,
For blushing cheeks are made by guilt,
And fear shows by turning pale white:
So if she is afraid or guilty,
You wouldn't be able to tell,
Since her cheeks will appear the same
As her normal look.
A dangerous rhyme, master, that argues against
White and red.

DON ADRIANO DE ARMADO
Is there not a ballad, boy, of the King and the Beggar?

Isn't there a ballad, boy, of the King and the Beggar?

MOTH
The world was very guilty of such a ballad some three ages since: but I think now 'tis not to be found; or, if it were, it would neither serve for the writing nor the tune.

The world was very guilty for making a ballad like that About three ages ago: but I think now it can't be Found; or, if it were, it wouldn't do for The writing or the tune.

DON ADRIANO DE ARMADO
I will have that subject newly writ o'er, that I may
example my digression by some mighty precedent.
Boy, I do love that country girl that I took in the park with the rational hind Costard: she deserves well.

I will have that ballad written anew, so that I can
See my deviation in a forceful example from the past.
Boy, I have fallen in love with that country girl that I arrested in the Park with the lowly Costard: she deserves better.

MOTH
[Aside] To be whipped; and yet a better love than
my master.

[Aside] Deserves to be whipped; and yet deserves a better love than My master.

DON ADRIANO DE ARMADO
Sing, boy; my spirit grows heavy in love.

Sing, boy; my mood grows heavy with love.

MOTH
And that's great marvel, loving a light wench.

And that's a great wonder, since you love a light wench.

DON ADRIANO DE ARMADO
I say, sing.

I'm telling you to sing.

MOTH
Forbear till this company be past.

Wait until after these people leave.

Enter DULL, COSTARD, and JAQUENETTA

DULL
Sir, the duke's pleasure is, that you keep Costard safe: and you must suffer him to take no delight nor no penance; but a' must fast three days a week.
For this damsel, I must keep her at the park: she is allowed for the day-woman. Fare you well.

Sir, what the duke wants is for you to keep Costard Safe: and you must make sure he has no enjoyment Or any punishment; but he must fast for three days a week.
For this damsel, I must keep her at the park: she Has been accepted to be the day-woman. Goodbye.

DON ADRIANO DE ARMADO
I do betray myself with blushing. Maid!

I'm betraying myself by blushing. Maid!

JAQUENETTA
Man?

Man?

DON ADRIANO DE ARMADO
I will visit thee at the lodge.

I will visit you at the lodge.

JAQUENETTA
That's hereby.

That's around here.

DON ADRIANO DE ARMADO
I know where it is situate.

I know where it is.

JAQUENETTA
Lord, how wise you are!

Lord, you are so wise!

DON ADRIANO DE ARMADO
I will tell thee wonders.

I will tell you wonders.

JAQUENETTA
With that face?

With that face?

DON ADRIANO DE ARMADO
I love thee.

I love you.

JAQUENETTA
So I heard you say.

So I heard you say.

DON ADRIANO DE ARMADO
And so, farewell.

And so, farewell.

JAQUENETTA
Fair weather after you!

May you have fair weather!

DULL
Come, Jaquenetta, away!

Come, Jaquenetta, let's go!

Exeunt DULL and JAQUENETTA

DON ADRIANO DE ARMADO
Villain, thou shalt fast for thy offences ere thou
be pardoned.

Scoundrel, you will fast for your offences before
you Will be pardoned.

COSTARD
Well, sir, I hope, when I do it, I shall do it on a
full stomach.

Well, sir, I hope that when I do it, I will do it on
a Full stomach.

DON ADRIANO DE ARMADO
Thou shalt be heavily punished.

You will be punished heavily.

COSTARD
I am more bound to you than your fellows, for
they
are but lightly rewarded.

I am more bound to you than your men, since
they
Are only lightly rewarded.

DON ADRIANO DE ARMADO
Take away this villain; shut him up.

Take this miscreant away; shut him up.

MOTH
Come, you transgressing slave; away!

Come on, you misbehaving slave, let's go!

COSTARD
Let me not be pent up, sir: I will fast, being
loose.

Please don't lock me up, sir: I will fast even if
I'm let loose.

MOTH
No, sir; that were fast and loose: thou shalt to

No, sir; that would be too easy: you're going to

prison.

prison.

COSTARD
Well, if ever I do see the merry days of desolation
that I have seen, some shall see.

Well, if I ever see the happy days of misery and lonliness
That I have seen, they'll see.

MOTH
What shall some see?

What do you mean they'll see? What will they see?

COSTARD
Nay, nothing, Master Moth, but what they look upon.
It is not for prisoners to be too silent in their words; and therefore I will say nothing: I thank God I have as little patience as another man; and therefore I can be quiet.

Oh, nothing, Master Moth, except what they look at.
Prisoners can never be too silent in their Words; and so I will say nothing: I thank God that I have as little patience as another man; and So I can be quiet.

Exeunt MOTH and COSTARD

DON ADRIANO DE ARMADO
I do affect the very ground, which is base, where her shoe, which is baser, guided by her foot, which
is basest, doth tread. I shall be forsworn, which is a great argument of falsehood, if I love. And how can that be true love which is falsely attempted? Love is a familiar; Love is a devil: there is no evil angel but Love. Yet was Samson so
tempted, and he had an excellent strength; yet was
Solomon so seduced, and he had a very good wit.
Cupid's butt-shaft is too hard for Hercules' club; and therefore too much odds for a Spaniard's rapier.
The first and second cause will not serve my turn;
the passado he respects not, the duello he regards
not: his disgrace is to be called boy; but his glory is to subdue men. Adieu, valour! rust rapier!
be still, drum! for your manager is in love; yea, he loveth. Assist me, some extemporal god of

I do love the very ground, which is lowly, where Her shoe, which is even lower, guided by her foot, which
Is the lowest, has tread. I shall be breaking my oaths, which Is a great proof of being untrue, if I love her. And How can a love be true that is falsely Attempted? Love is a demon animal; Love is a devil: There is no evil angel except Love. Yet even Samson
Was tempted, and he had enormous strength; and even
Solomon was seduced, and he was very smart. Cupid's arrow is too hard even for Hercules' club;
And therefore much too strong for a Spaniard's sword.
The first and the second reason will do me no good;
He doesn't respect the cutting lunge, he doesn't respect the one-on-one duel:
He is disgraced to be called a boy; but his victory is to conquer men. Goodbye, valour! Collect rust, sword!
be still, war drum! Because your owner is in love; truly he loves. If there's some god of

rhyme,
for I am sure I shall turn sonnet. Devise, wit;
write, pen; for I am for whole volumes in folio.

Exit

impromptu poetry, help me,
I'm sure I will be writing a sonnet. Think, wits;
Write, pen; I'm ready to write whole volumes of
pages.

ACT II

SCENE I. The same.

Enter the PRINCESS of France, ROSALINE, MARIA, KATHARINE, BOYET, Lords, and other Attendants

BOYET

Now, madam, summon up your dearest spirits:
Consider who the king your father sends,
To whom he sends, and what's his embassy:
Yourself, held precious in the world's esteem,
To parley with the sole inheritor
Of all perfections that a man may owe,
Matchless Navarre; the plea of no less weight
Than Aquitaine, a dowry for a queen.
Be now as prodigal of all dear grace
As Nature was in making graces dear
When she did starve the general world beside
And prodigally gave them all to you.

Now, madam, summon up your most affectionate mood: Think about who the king, your father is sending, Who he sends, and what's his mission: You yourself, held precious and well-regarded by the world, To negotiate with the sole inheritor Of all perfections that a man can own, Navarre, there is nothing like it; and the plea has no less weight Thank Aquitaine, a dowry for a queen. Be as lavish with affection and grace As Nature was in making graces dear When she starved the whole world of them And lavishly gave them all to you.

PRINCESS

Good Lord Boyet, my beauty, though but mean,
Needs not the painted flourish of your praise:
Beauty is bought by judgement of the eye,
Not utter'd by base sale of chapmen's tongues:
I am less proud to hear you tell my worth
Than you much willing to be counted wise
In spending your wit in the praise of mine.
But now to task the tasker: good Boyet,
You are not ignorant, all-telling fame
Doth noise abroad, Navarre hath made a vow,
Till painful study shall outwear three years,
No woman may approach his silent court:
Therefore to's seemeth it a needful course,
Before we enter his forbidden gates,
To know his pleasure; and in that behalf,
Bold of your worthiness, we single you
As our best-moving fair solicitor.
Tell him, the daughter of the King of France,
On serious business, craving quick dispatch,
Importunes personal conference with his grace:
Haste, signify so much; while we attend,
Like humble-visaged suitors, his high will.

My good Lord Boyet, though I have very little beauty, You don't need to paint it with the flourish of your praise: Beauty is bought by the judgement of others' eyes, Not by the cheap selling of a peddler's tongue: I am less proud to hear you talk about my worth Than you are proud to be called wise For spending your wit in the praise of mine. But now to give the dutiful a duty: good Boyet, You are not ignorant, fame which tells all Has been making noise abroad, I have heard that Navarre has made a vow, To painfully study for three years, And until then no woman can approach his silent court: So it seems that what we need to do, Before we enter his forbidden gates, To know what he wants us to do: and for that purpose, Assured of your worthiness, we have singled you out To be the most moving solicitor to our cause. Tell him, the daughter of the King of France, On serious business, craves a quick word, Begs a personal conference with his grace: Go quickly, tell him this; while we await, Like humble-faced suitors, his high will.

BOYET

Proud of employment, willingly I go.

Proud to have been chosen, I go willingly.

PRINCESS
All pride is willing pride, and yours is so.

All pride is willing and eager, and yours is too.

Exit BOYET

Who are the votaries, my loving lords,
That are vow-fellows with this virtuous duke?

Who are the avowed, my loving lords,
Who are the men who also took oaths with this
virtuous duke?

First Lord
Lord Longaville is one.

One of them is Lord Longaville.

PRINCESS
Know you the man?

Do you know him?

MARIA
I know him, madam: at a marriage-feast,
Between Lord Perigort and the beauteous heir
Of Jaques Falconbridge, solemnized
In Normandy, saw I this Longaville:
A man of sovereign parts he is esteem'd;
Well fitted in arts, glorious in arms:
Nothing becomes him ill that he would well.
The only soil of his fair virtue's gloss,
If virtue's gloss will stain with any soil,
Is a sharp wit matched with too blunt a will;
Whose edge hath power to cut, whose will still
wills
It should none spare that come within his power.

I know him, madam: at a wedding
Between Lord Perigort and the beautiful heir
Of Jaques Falconbridge, officiated
In Normandy, I saw this Longaville:
A man of royal parts he is well-respected:
Skilled at the arts, glorious in combat:
Nothing makes him look bad if he doesn't want
it to. The only stain on his honest virtue's gloss
If virtue's gloss can be stained,
Is that his sharp wit is matched with self-control
that is too blunt;
The edge of which can still cut, if he wills,
It will spare no one that comes within his power.

PRINCESS
Some merry mocking lord, belike; is't so?

He sounds like a cheerful, mocking sort of lord;
is that right?

MARIA
They say so most that most his humours know.

The people that know him most say so.

PRINCESS
Such short-lived wits do wither as they grow.
Who are the rest?

Short-lived wits like that wither as they grow.
Who are the rest?

KATHARINE
The young Dumain, a well-accomplished youth,
Of all that virtue love for virtue loved:
Most power to do most harm, least knowing ill;
For he hath wit to make an ill shape good,
And shape to win grace though he had no wit.
I saw him at the Duke Alencon's once;

The young Dumain, a well-accomplished young
man. He is everything that the virtuous love:
He has the most power to do the most harm,
least knowing wrong; For he has wit to make
something bad seem good, And has the form to
win grace if he has no wit. I saw him at the

And much too little of that good I saw
Is my report to his great worthiness.

ROSALINE
Another of these students at that time
Was there with him, if I have heard a truth.
Biron they call him; but a merrier man,
Within the limit of becoming mirth,
I never spent an hour's talk withal:
His eye begets occasion for his wit;
For every object that the one doth catch
The other turns to a mirth-moving jest,
Which his fair tongue, conceit's expositor,
Delivers in such apt and gracious words
That aged ears play truant at his tales
And younger hearings are quite ravished;
So sweet and voluble is his discourse.

PRINCESS
God bless my ladies! are they all in love,
That every one her own hath garnished
With such bedecking ornaments of praise?

First Lord
Here comes Boyet.

Re-enter BOYET

PRINCESS
Now, what admittance, lord?

BOYET
Navarre had notice of your fair approach;
And he and his competitors in oath
Were all address'd to meet you, gentle lady,
Before I came. Marry, thus much I have learnt:
He rather means to lodge you in the field,
Like one that comes here to besiege his court,
Than seek a dispensation for his oath,
To let you enter his unpeopled house.
Here comes Navarre.

Enter FERDINAND, LONGAVILLE, DUMAIN, BIRON, and Attendan

FERDINAND

*Duke Alencon's once; And I saw much too little
of that good That is my report on his great
worthiness.*

*Another of these students at the same time
Was there with him, if I have heard true.
Biron, they call him; but a more cheerful man,
Withing the limit of becoming laughter,
I never spent an hour's talk with in my whole
life: His eye brings about the cause for his wit;
For every object that the eye catches
His wit turns into a laughter-inducing joke,
Which his fine tongue, which is like a
commentator of fanciful expressions, Delivers
with such apt and gracious words That older
ears cannot keep up with his tales And younger
listeners are completely carried away by; So
sweet and talkative is his conversation.*

*God bless my ladies! Are they all in love,
So that every one has decorated her own
With such ornaments and compliments of
praise?*

Here comes Boyet.

Are we to be admitted, lord?

*Navarre was notified of your approach;
And he and the others who took oaths together
Were all addressed to meet you, gentle lady,
Before I came. This is as much as I have
learned: It seems he means to let you stay in the
field, Like someone who comes here to take over
his court, Than to make an exception for his
oath, So that he can let you enter his empty
house. Here comes Navarre.*

Fair princess, welcome to the court of Navarre.   **PRINCESS**

PRINCESS
'Fair' I give you back again; and 'welcome' I have
not yet: the roof of this court is too high to be
yours; and welcome to the wide fields too base
to be mine.

FERDINAND
You shall be welcome, madam, to my court.

PRINCESS
I will be welcome, then: conduct me thither.

FERDINAND
Hear me, dear lady; I have sworn an oath.

PRINCESS
Our Lady help my lord! he'll be forsworn.

FERDINAND
Not for the world, fair madam, by my will.

PRINCESS
Why, will shall break it; will and nothing else.

FERDINAND
Your ladyship is ignorant what it is.

PRINCESS
Were my lord so, his ignorance were wise,
Where now his knowledge must prove
ignorance.
I hear your grace hath sworn out house-keeping:
Tis deadly sin to keep that oath, my lord,
And sin to break it.
But pardon me. I am too sudden-bold:
To teach a teacher ill beseemeth me.
Vouchsafe to read the purpose of my coming,
And suddenly resolve me in my suit.

FERDINAND
Madam, I will, if suddenly I may.

Fair princess, welcome to the court of Navarre.

You can take back 'fair': and as for 'welcome' I have
Not had any yet: the roof of this court is too
high to be yours; and the welcome to the wide
fields is too lowly to be mine.

You will be welcome, madam, to my court.

I would like to be welcomed, then: take me there.

Listen, dear lady; I have sworn an oath.

Oh Mary, help my lord! He'll break his oath!

Not for the world, fair lady, by my will.

Well, your will shall break it; will and nothing else.

Your ladyship doesn't know what it is.

If my lord was so, his ignorance would be wise,
Where now his knowledge must prove ignorance.
I hear your grace has sworn out house-keeping:
It's a deadly sin to keep that oath, my lord,
And a sin to break it.
But excuse me. I am too bold all of a sudden:
To teach a teacher doesn't become me.
Graciously condescend to read the purpose of
my coming here, And soon settle my petition.

Madam, I will, and soon if I can

You will the sooner, that I were away;
For you'll prove perjured if you make me stay.

BIRON
Did not I dance with you in Brabant once?

ROSALINE
Did not I dance with you in Brabant once?

BIRON
I know you did.

ROSALINE
How needless was it then to ask the question!

BIRON
You must not be so quick.

ROSALINE
'Tis 'long of you that spur me with such
questions.

BIRON
Your wit's too hot, it speeds too fast, 'twill tire.

ROSALINE
Not till it leave the rider in the mire.

BIRON
What time o' day?

ROSALINE
The hour that fools should ask.

BIRON
Now fair befall your mask!

ROSALINE
Fair fall the face it covers!

BIRON
And send you many lovers!

ROSALINE
Amen, so you be none.

You should do it sooner, so that I can leave;
Since you'll be breaking your oath if you make
me stay.

Didn't I dance with you in Brabant once?

Didn't I dance with you in Brabant once?

I know you did.

Then it was needless to ask the question!

You shouldn't be so hasty.

You're taking up a lot of time asking such
questions.

Your wit is too hot, it speeds too fast, it will get
tired.

Not before it leaves its rider stuck in the mud of
the swamps.

At what time of day?

The hour that fools would ask.

And now your mask becomes beautiful!

Beautiful becomes the face that it covers!

And send you many lovers!

Amen, so you won't be one.

BIRON
Nay, then will I be gone.

FERDINAND
Madam, your father here doth intimate
The payment of a hundred thousand crowns;
Being but the one half of an entire sum
Disbursed by my father in his wars.
But say that he or we, as neither have,
Received that sum, yet there remains unpaid
A hundred thousand more; in surety of the
which,
One part of Aquitaine is bound to us,
Although not valued to the money's worth.
If then the king your father will restore
But that one half which is unsatisfied,
We will give up our right in Aquitaine,
And hold fair friendship with his majesty.
But that, it seems, he little purposeth,
For here he doth demand to have repaid
A hundred thousand crowns; and not demands,
On payment of a hundred thousand crowns,
To have his title live in Aquitaine;
Which we much rather had depart withal
And have the money by our father lent
Than Aquitaine so gelded as it is.
Dear Princess, were not his requests so far
From reason's yielding, your fair self should
make
A yielding 'gainst some reason in my breast
And go well satisfied to France again.

PRINCESS
You do the king my father too much wrong
And wrong the reputation of your name,
In so unseeming to confess receipt
Of that which hath so faithfully been paid.

FERDINAND
I do protest I never heard of it;
And if you prove it, I'll repay it back
Or yield up Aquitaine.

PRINCESS
We arrest your word.

Boyet, you can produce acquittances

No, then I will be gone.

Madam, your father indicates here
That there will be a payment of a hundred
thousand crowns; That being only half of the
entire sum That my father gave in his wars.
But let's say the he or we, as neither of us have,
Received that sum, there remains unpaid
A hundred thousand morel ; which will be
insured
By trading one part of Aquitaine to us,
Although it is not valued to that money's worth.
If the king your father will give return
Just the one half that has yet to be paid,
We will give up our claim in Aquitaine,
And have a fine friendship with his majesty.
But that, it seems, is hardly his purpose,
Here he demands to have us repay him
A hundred thousand crowns; and does not
demand, On payment of a hundred thousand
crowns, To have claim of Aquitaine;
Which we would much rather part with
And have the money lent by our father
Than to have Aquitaine as broken as it is.
Dear Princess, if his requests weren't so
Unreasonable, your good self could make
An argument agains some reason in my breast
And go well satisfied to France again.

You do the king my father too much wrong
And do wrong to the reputation of your name,
By saying that you never received
That which has been so faithfully paid.

I must protest that I never heard of that;
And if you prove it, I'll repay it back
Or give up Aquitaine.

We will take you at you word.
Boyet, you can produce receipts

For such a sum from special officers
Of Charles his father.

FERDINAND
Satisfy me so.

BOYET
So please your grace, the packet is not come
Where that and other specialties are bound:
To-morrow you shall have a sight of them.

FERDINAND
It shall suffice me: at which interview
All liberal reason I will yield unto.
Meantime receive such welcome at my hand
As honour without breach of honour may
Make tender of to thy true worthiness:
You may not come, fair princess, in my gates;
But here without you shall be so received
As you shall deem yourself lodged in my heart,
Though so denied fair harbour in my house.
Your own good thoughts excuse me, and
farewell:
To-morrow shall we visit you again.

PRINCESS
Sweet health and fair desires consort your grace!

FERDINAND
Thy own wish wish I thee in every place!

Exit

BIRON
Lady, I will commend you to mine own heart.

ROSALINE
Pray you, do my commendations; I would be
glad to see it.

BIRON
I would you heard it groan.

ROSALINE
Is the fool sick?

For that payment from special officers
Of Charles his father.

Satisfy me by showing them to me.

Well, your grace, the packet has not come
Where that and other things are bound to go:
You will be able to see them tomorrow.

That will suffice: and at the interview
I will give in to whatever is reasonable.
In the meantime, receive as much welcome at
my hand As my honor, without breaching my
honor, can Offer to your true worthiness:
You may not come, beautiful princess, in my
gates; But here outside you shall be so well
received That you will consider yourself as
staying the night in my own heart, Though you
are denied good shelter in my house. Your own
good thoughts will excuse me, and goodbye:
Tomorrow we will visit you again.

Sweet health and good desires be your grace's
companions!

Your own wish I wish back to you in every way!

Lady, I will praise you to my own heart.

Please go ahead, say my praises; I would be
glad to see it.

You would probably hear it groan.

Is the fool sick?

BIRON
Sick at the heart.

Heartsick.

ROSALINE
Alack, let it blood.

Oh no! you should bleed it.

BIRON
Would that do it good?

Would that do it good?

ROSALINE
My physic says 'ay.'

My doctor says "Aye."

BIRON
Will you prick't with your eye?

Will you prick it with your eye?

ROSALINE
No point, with my knife.

No, with my knife.

BIRON
Now, God save thy life!

Now, God save your life!

ROSALINE
And yours from long living!

And yours from living long!

BIRON
I cannot stay thanksgiving.

I can't stay giving thanks.

Retiring

DUMAIN
Sir, I pray you, a word: what lady is that same?

Sir, can I ask you something: who is that lady?

BOYET
The heir of Alencon, Katharine her name.

The heir of Alencon, her name is Katharine.

DUMAIN
A gallant lady. Monsieur, fare you well.

A brave lady. Monsieur, goodbye.

Exit

LONGAVILLE
I beseech you a word: what is she in the white?

I beg a word of you: what is she in the white?

BOYET
A woman sometimes, an you saw her in the light.

A woman sometimes, and you saw her in the light.

LONGAVILLE
Perchance light in the light. I desire her name.

Perhaps radiant in the light. I want her name.

BOYET
She hath but one for herself; to desire that were a shame.

She only has one and that's for herself; to want that would be a shame.

LONGAVILLE
Pray you, sir, whose daughter?

Please sir, I mean whose daughter is she?

BOYET
Her mother's, I have heard.

Her mother's, I have heard.

LONGAVILLE
God's blessing on your beard!

My God man!

BOYET
Good sir, be not offended.
She is an heir of Falconbridge.

Good sir, don't get offended.
She is an heir of Falconbridge.

LONGAVILLE
Nay, my choler is ended.
She is a most sweet lady.

No, my upset has ended.
She is a very sweet lady.

BOYET
Not unlike, sir, that may be.

That may be, sir.

Exit LONGAVILLE

BIRON
What's her name in the cap?

What's her name, in the cap?

BOYET
Rosaline, by good hap.

Rosaline, by good luck.

BIRON
Is she wedded or no?

Is she married or no?

BOYET
To her will, sir, or so.

To her own will, sir.

BIRON
You are welcome, sir: adieu.

You are very welcome here, sir: goodbye

BOYET

Farewell to me, sir, and welcome to you.

Goodbye to me sir, and welcome to you.

Exit BIRON

MARIA

That last is Biron, the merry madcap lord:
Not a word with him but a jest.

That last one was Biron, the cheerful and reckless lord: Never just words with him but jokes.

BOYET
And every jest but a word.

And every joke is a word.

PRINCESS
It was well done of you to take him at his word.

It was well done for you to take everything he said literally.

BOYET
I was as willing to grapple as he was to board.

I was as willing to wrestle words with him as he was to get information.

MARIA
Two hot sheeps, marry.

Two angry rams, how funny.

BOYET
And wherefore not ships?
No sheep, sweet lamb, unless we feed on your lips.

*And how come we can't be ships?
Not rams, sweet lamb, unless we feed on your lips.*

MARIA
You sheep, and I pasture: shall that finish the jest?

You are sheep and I'm a pasture: does that finish the joke?

BOYET
So you grant pasture for me.

So you grant me pasture.

Offering to kiss her

MARIA
Not so, gentle beast:
My lips are no common, though several they be.

*Not at all, gentle beast:
My lips are not for general use, though there are several.*

BOYET
Belonging to whom?

Who do they belong to?

MARIA
To my fortunes and me.

To my fortunes and me.

PRINCESS

Good wits will be jangling; but, gentles, agree:
This civil war of wits were much better used
On Navarre and his book-men; for here 'tis
abused.

BOYET
If my observation, which very seldom lies,
By the heart's still rhetoric disclosed with eyes,
Deceive me not now, Navarre is infected.

PRINCESS
With what?

BOYET
With that which we lovers entitle affected.

PRINCESS
Your reason?

BOYET
Why, all his behaviors did make their retire
To the court of his eye, peeping thorough desire:
His heart, like an agate, with your print
impress'd,
Proud with his form, in his eye pride express'd:
His tongue, all impatient to speak and not see,
Did stumble with haste in his eyesight to be;
All senses to that sense did make their repair,
To feel only looking on fairest of fair:
Methought all his senses were lock'd in his eye,
As jewels in crystal for some prince to buy;
Who, tendering their own worth from where
they were glass'd,
Did point you to buy them, along as you pass'd:
His face's own margent did quote such amazes
That all eyes saw his eyes enchanted with gazes.
I'll give you Aquitaine and all that is his,
An you give him for my sake but one loving
kiss.

PRINCESS
Come to our pavilion: Boyet is disposed.

BOYET
But to speak that in words which his eye hath

*This is a good banter of wits; but gentle ones,
we must agree: This war between us of wits
would be much better used On Navarre and his
study-men; for here it is misused.*

*If my observations, which very seldom lies,
Read the heart's persuasion, uncovered by my
eyes, Don't deceive me now, I would say that
Navarre is infected.*

With what?

With what we lovers call affection.

What makes you say that?

*Well, all his behaviors retreated
To the court of his eye, seeing complete desire:
His heart like an agate stone, has been marked
with your print,
Proud with his form, his eyes expressed pride;
His tongue, all impatient to speak and not see,
Did stumble with his rush to see you;
All of his senses retreated to the sense of sight
So that they could all only feel looking at the
most beautiful beauty: It seemed to me that all
his senses were fixed in his eyes, Like jewels in
crystal for some prince to buy; Who, offering
their own worth from inside their glass,
Did point at you to buy them, as you passed
along: You could tell by his face that he was
amazed And all eyes saw his eyes enchanted
with gazes. I'll give you Aquitaine and
everything he owns, If, for my sake, you give him
one loving kiss.*

Come to our pavilion: Boyet is done for the day.

I only spoke in words that which his eyes

disclosed.
I only have made a mouth of his eye,
By adding a tongue which I know will not lie.

ROSALINE
Thou art an old love-monger and speakest
skilfully.

MARIA
He is Cupid's grandfather and learns news of
him.

ROSALINE
Then was Venus like her mother, for her father
is but grim.

BOYET
Do you hear, my mad wenches?

MARIA
No.

BOYET
What then, do you see?

ROSALINE
Ay, our way to be gone.

BOYET
You are too hard for me.

Exeunt

Disclosed,
I have only made a mouth of his eye,
By adding a tongue that I know will not lie.

You are an old matchmaker, and speak
skillfully.

He is Cupid's grandfather and learns news
about love from him.

Then Venus was like her mother, for her father
is but girm.

Do you hear what I'm saying, you crazy girls?

No.

What then, do you see?

The way out of here.

Oh, I give up.

ACT III

SCENE I.

Enter DON ADRIANO DE ARMADO and MOTH

DON ADRIANO DE ARMADO
Warble, child; make passionate my sense of hearing.

Sing, child; make my ears feel passion.

MOTH
Concolinel.

Concolinel.

Singing

DON ADRIANO DE ARMADO
Sweet air! Go, tenderness of years; take this key, give enlargement to the swain, bring him festinately
hither: I must employ him in a letter to my love.

Sweet song! Go, young one; take this key,
Release the country boy, bring him quickly
Here: I must send him to take a letter to my love.

MOTH
Master, will you win your love with a French brawl?

Master, will you win your love with a French dance?

DON ADRIANO DE ARMADO
How meanest thou? brawling in French?

How do you mean? Dancing in French?

MOTH
No, my complete master: but to jig off a tune at the tongue's end, canary to it with your feet, humour
it with turning up your eyelids, sigh a note and sing a note, sometime through the throat, as if you
swallowed love with singing love, sometime through
the nose, as if you snuffed up love by smelling love; with your hat penthouse-like o'er the shop of
your eyes; with your arms crossed on your thin-belly
doublet like a rabbit on a spit; or your hands in your pocket like a man after the old painting; and
keep not too long in one tune, but a snip and away.

No, my perfect master: but to do a jig off a tune
at The tongue's end, dance to it with your feet, humor
It by turning up your eyelids, sigh a note and
Sing a note, sometimes through the throat, as if you
Swallowed love with singing love, sometimes through
The nose, as if you sniffed up love by smelling
Love; with your hat like a balcony over the shop of
Your eyes; with your arms crossed on your thin belly
Jacket like a rabbit on a spit; or your hands in
Your pocket like a man in an old painting; and
Don't keep singing one tune for too long, but do
snippets of different songs.

These are complements, these are humours;
these
betray nice wenches, that would be betrayed
without
these; and make them men of note--do you note
me?--that most are affected to these.

DON ADRIANO DE ARMADO
How hast thou purchased this experience?

MOTH
By my penny of observation.

DON ADRIANO DE ARMADO
But O,--but O,--

MOTH
'The hobby-horse is forgot.'

DON ADRIANO DE ARMADO
Callest thou my love 'hobby-horse'?

MOTH
No, master; the hobby-horse is but a colt, and
your
love perhaps a hackney. But have you forgot
your love?

DON ADRIANO DE ARMADO
Almost I had.

MOTH
Negligent student! learn her by heart.

DON ADRIANO DE ARMADO
By heart and in heart, boy.

MOTH
And out of heart, master: all those three I will
prove.

DON ADRIANO DE ARMADO
What wilt thou prove?

MOTH

*These are gentlemanly accomplishments, these
are amusing; these
Betray coy girls, that would be betrayed without
These; and make them noteworthy men—are you
noting
What I'm saying?—that are the most drawn to
these.*

Have you yourself purchased this experience?

With my penny of observation.

But oh,--- but oh,---

'The hobby-horse has been forgotten.'

Are you calling my love a 'prostitute'?

*No, master, the prostitute is only a slut, and
your
Love is maybe just promiscuous. But have you
forgot your love's name?*

I almost did.

Neglectful student! Learn her by heart.

By heart and in heart, boy.

*And out of heart, master: all those three I will
prove.*

What will you prove?

A man, if I live; and this, by, in, and without, upon
the instant: by heart you love her, because your heart cannot come by her; in heart you love her, because your heart is in love with her; and out of heart you love her, being out of heart that you cannot enjoy her.

DON ADRIANO DE ARMADO
I am all these three.

MOTH
And three times as much more, and yet nothing at
all.

DON ADRIANO DE ARMADO
Fetch hither the swain: he must carry me a letter.

MOTH
A message well sympathized; a horse to be ambassador
for an ass.

DON ADRIANO DE ARMADO
Ha, ha! what sayest thou?

MOTH
Marry, sir, you must send the ass upon the horse,
for he is very slow-gaited. But I go.

DON ADRIANO DE ARMADO
The way is but short: away!

MOTH
As swift as lead, sir.

DON ADRIANO DE ARMADO
The meaning, pretty ingenious?
Is not lead a metal heavy, dull, and slow?

MOTH
Minime, honest master; or rather, master, no.

DON ADRIANO DE ARMADO

I will prove to be a man, if I live; and this, by, in, and without, on
The instant: by heart you love her, because your heart cannot get close to her; you love her in your heart Because your heart is in love with her; and out of Heart you love her, being out of spirits since you Cannot enjoy her.

I am all these three.

And three times as much more, and yet nothing at
All.

Fetch me the country boy: he must carry a letter for me.

A message well matched; a horse to be an ambassdor
For an ass.

Ha, Ha! What did you say to me?

Only, sir, that you must send that ass on horseback,
Since he is so slow. But I'll go.

The way is very short: go!

As fast as lead, sir.

And what's the meaning of that, smart guy?
Isn't lead a heavy metal, dull and slow?

Not at all, master; or rather, no, master.

I say lead is slow.

I say lead is slow.

MOTH
You are too swift, sir, to say so:
Is that lead slow which is fired from a gun?

You are too swift to say so, sir.
Is lead slow that is fired from a gun?

DON ADRIANO DE ARMADO
Sweet smoke of rhetoric!
He reputes me a cannon; and the bullet, that's he:
I shoot thee at the swain.

Sweet smoke of rhetoric!
He calls me a cannon; and him a bullet:
I shoot you at the country boy!

MOTH
Thump then and I flee.

"Boom" then and I run away.

Exit

DON ADRIANO DE ARMADO
A most acute juvenal; voluble and free of grace!
By thy favour, sweet welkin, I must sigh in thy face:
Most rude melancholy, valour gives thee place.
My herald is return'd.

A very keen young man; quick-witted and
charming! By your favor, sweet sky, I must sigh
in your face:
And such rude melancholy, courage gives way
to you. My herald has retunred.

Re-enter MOTH with COSTARD

MOTH
A wonder, master! here's a costard broken in a shin.

It's a mystery, master! Here is Costard, with a
bruised shin.

DON ADRIANO DE ARMADO
Some enigma, some riddle: come, thy l'envoy; begin.

Some puzzle, some riddle: come, tell us your
l'envoy.

COSTARD
No enigma, no riddle, no l'envoy; no salve in the mail, sir: O, sir, plantain, a plain plantain! No l'envoy, no l'envoy; no salve, sir, but a plantain!

No puzzle, no riddle, no l'envoy; there's no
salve in the Mail, sir: O, sir, an ointment, a
plain ointment! No l'envoy, no l'envoy; no
salve, sir, but an ointment!

DON ADRIANO DE ARMADO
By virtue, thou enforcest laughter; thy silly thought my spleen; the heaving of my lungs provokes
me to ridiculous smiling. O, pardon me, my stars!

My word, you make me laugh; my spleen
Thinks you're silly; the heaving of my lungs
provokes
Me to smile ridiculously. O, pardon me, my
stars!

Doth the inconsiderate take salve for l'envoy,
and
the word l'envoy for a salve?

Does the fool think that ointment means l'envoy, and
The word l'envoy means ointment?

MOTH
Do the wise think them other? is not l'envoy a
salve?

Do the wise think that they're not? Isn't a
l'envoy an ointment?

DON ADRIANO DE ARMADO
No, page: it is an epilogue or discourse, to make
plain
Some obscure precedence that hath tofore been
sain.
I will example it:
The fox, the ape, and the humble-bee,
Were still at odds, being but three.
There's the moral. Now the l'envoy.

No, young one: it is an epilogue or
conversation, to make understood
Some hidden moral.
Here's an example:
The fox, the ape, and the humble bee,
Were still at odds, since there were only three of them.
There's the moral. Now the l'envoy.

MOTH
I will add the l'envoy. Say the moral again.

I will add the l'envoy. Say the moral again.

DON ADRIANO DE ARMADO
The fox, the ape, and the humble-bee,
Were still at odds, being but three.

The fox, the ape, and the humble bee,
Were still at odds, since there were only three of them.

MOTH
Until the goose came out of door,
And stay'd the odds by adding four.
Now will I begin your moral, and do you follow
with
my l'envoy.
The fox, the ape, and the humble-bee,
Were still at odds, being but three.

Until the goose came out the door,
And fixed the odds by making them four.
Now I will begin your moral, and you follow
with
My l'envoy.
The fox, the ape, and the humble bee,
Were still at odds, since there were only three of them.

DON ADRIANO DE ARMADO
Until the goose came out of door,
Staying the odds by adding four.

Until the goose came out the door,
And fixed the odds by making them four.

MOTH
A good l'envoy, ending in the goose: would you
desire more?

A good l'envoy ending in the goose: would you
Desire more?

COSTARD
The boy hath sold him a bargain, a goose, that's
flat.
Sir, your pennyworth is good, an your goose be

The boy has sold him a bargain, a goose, that's
flat.
Sir, your contribution is good, and your goose is

fat.
To sell a bargain well is as cunning as fast and loose:
Let me see; a fat l'envoy; ay, that's a fat goose.

DON ADRIANO DE ARMADO
Come hither, come hither. How did this argument begin?

MOTH
By saying that a costard was broken in a shin.
Then call'd you for the l'envoy.

COSTARD
True, and I for a plantain: thus came your argument in;
Then the boy's fat l'envoy, the goose that you bought;
And he ended the market.

DON ADRIANO DE ARMADO
But tell me; how was there a costard broken in a shin?

MOTH
I will tell you sensibly.

COSTARD
Thou hast no feeling of it, Moth: I will speak that l'envoy:
I Costard, running out, that was safely within,
Fell over the threshold and broke my shin.

DON ADRIANO DE ARMADO
We will talk no more of this matter.

COSTARD
Till there be more matter in the shin.

DON ADRIANO DE ARMADO
Sirrah Costard, I will enfranchise thee.

COSTARD
O, marry me to one Frances: I smell some l'envoy,

fat.
To sell a bargain well is as cunning as it is fast and loose.
Let me see, a fat l'envoy; yes, that's a fat goose.

Come now, come now. How did this argument begin?

By saying that Costard had a broken shin.
Then you asked for the l'envoy.

True, and I asked for an ointment: then your Argument started;
Then the boy's fat l'envoy, the goose that you bought;
And he ended the market.

But tell me; how did Costard break his shin?

I will tell you.

You can't even feel it, Moth: I will speak that l'envoy:
I, Costard, running out, from where I was safely within,
Fell over the doorway and broke my shin.

We will talk no more of this matter.

Until there is more matter in the shin.

Slave Costard, I will free you.

O, marry me to Frances: I smell some l'envoy,

some goose, in this.

DON ADRIANO DE ARMADO
By my sweet soul, I mean setting thee at liberty,
enfreedoming thy person; thou wert immured,
restraincd, captivated, bound.

COSTARD
True, true; and now you will be my purgation
and let me loose.

DON ADRIANO DE ARMADO
I give thee thy liberty, set thee from durance;
and,
in lieu thereof, impose on thee nothing but this:
bear this significant

Giving a letter

to the country maid Jaquenetta:
there is remuneration; for the best ward of mine
honour is rewarding my dependents. Moth,
follow.

Exit

MOTH
Like the sequel, I. Signior Costard, adieu.

COSTARD
My sweet ounce of man's flesh! my incony Jew!

Exit MOTH

Now will I look to his remuneration.
Remuneration!
O, that's the Latin word for three farthings: three
farthings--remuneration.--'What's the price of
this
inkle?'--'One penny.'--'No, I'll give you a
remuneration:' why, it carries it. Remuneration!
why, it is a fairer name than French crown. I
will
never buy and sell out of this word.

Enter BIRON

Some goose, in this.

*By my sweet soul, I mean setting you free,
Freeing your person; you were confined,
Restrained, held captive, bound.*

*True, true; and now you will be my purification
and let me loose.*

*I give you your freedom, end your long
imprisonment; and
Instead of that, impose on you nothing but this:
Take this*

*To the country maid Jaquenetta:
There is remuneration; for the best guard of my
honor is rewarding my dependents. Moth, go
with him.*

*I will be like the sequel. Mister Costard,
goodbye.*

*You sweet ounce of man's flesh! You rare and
pretty Jew!*

*Now I will look for his remuneration.
Remuneration!
O, that's the Latin word for three pennies: three
Pennies—payment—'How much for this
Linen?'—'One cent.'—'No, I'll give you a
Remuneration:' it wins the day. Remuneration!
It's has a nicer ring to it that French crown. I
will
Never buy and sell without using this word.*

BIRON
O, my good knave Costard! exceedingly well met.

O, my young rogue Costard! Very good to see you.

COSTARD
Pray you, sir, how much carnation ribbon may a man
buy for a remuneration?

Please, sir, how much pink ribbon may a man buy for a remuneration?

BIRON
What is a remuneration?

What is a remuneration?

COSTARD
Marry, sir, halfpenny farthing.

Well, sir, three pennies.

BIRON
Why, then, three-farthing worth of silk.

Well, then, three pennies worth of silk.

COSTARD
I thank your worship: God be wi' you!

I thank you your worship: God be with you!

BIRON
Stay, slave; I must employ thee:
As thou wilt win my favour, good my knave,
Do one thing for me that I shall entreat.

Wait, slave; I need you to do something for me. If you want to win my good regard, my good rogue, Do this one thing for me that I ask.

COSTARD
When would you have it done, sir?

When do you need it done, sir?

BIRON
This afternoon.

This afternoon.

COSTARD
Well, I will do it, sir: fare you well.

Well, I will do it, sir: goodbye.

BIRON
Thou knowest not what it is.

You don't even know what it is.

COSTARD
I shall know, sir, when I have done it.

I will know, sir, when I have done it.

BIRON
Why, villain, thou must know first.

No, scoundrel, you must know what it is first.

COSTARD

I will come to your worship to-morrow morning.

BIRON
It must be done this afternoon.
Hark, slave, it is but this:
The princess comes to hunt here in the park,
And in her train there is a gentle lady;
When tongues speak sweetly, then they name
her name,
And Rosaline they call her: ask for her;
And to her white hand see thou do commend
This seal'd-up counsel. There's thy guerdon; go.

Giving him a shilling

COSTARD
Gardon, O sweet gardon! better than
remuneration,
a'leven-pence farthing better: most sweet
gardon! I
will do it sir, in print. Gardon! Remuneration!

Exit

BIRON
And I, forsooth, in love! I, that have been love's
whip;
A very beadle to a humorous sigh;
A critic, nay, a night-watch constable;
A domineering pedant o'er the boy;
Than whom no mortal so magnificent!
This whimpled, whining, purblind, wayward
boy;
This senior-junior, giant-dwarf, Dan Cupid;
Regent of love-rhymes, lord of folded arms,
The anointed sovereign of sighs and groans,
Liege of all loiterers and malcontents,
Dread prince of plackets, king of codpieces,
Sole imperator and great general
Of trotting 'paritors:--O my little heart:--
And I to be a corporal of his field,
And wear his colours like a tumbler's hoop!
What, I! I love! I sue! I seek a wife!
A woman, that is like a German clock,
Still a-repairing, ever out of frame,
And never going aright, being a watch,

I will come to you tomorrow morning, your
worship.

But it must be done this afternoon.
Listen, slave, it is only this:
The princess comes to hunt here in the park,
And with her there is a gently lady;
When tongues speak sweetly, then they say her
name,
And Rosaline they call her: ask for her;
And into her white hand see that you entrust
This sealed up private letter. There's your
guerdon; go.

Gardon, O sweet gardon! This is better than
remuneration,
Eleven pennies better: most sweet gardon! I
Will do it sir, most exactly. Gardon!
Remuneration!

And I, truly, in love! I, who has been love's
whip;
A parish officer, who whips any emotional sigh;
A critic, no, a night watch officer;
A domineering prude over the boy;
Than whom no mortal so magnificent!
This blindfolded, whining, completely blind,
wayward boy;
This older young one, giant-dwarf, Sir Cupid;
Regent of love-rhymes, lord of melancholy,
The anointed king of sighs and groans,
Lord of all loiterers and malcontents,
Dreaded prince of petticoats, kind of codpieces,
Sole commander and great general
Of trotting apparitors; --O my little heart:--
And for me to be a corporal of his field
And wear his colors like a clown!
What, I?! I love! I sue! I seek a wife!
A woman, that is like a German clock,
Always needing repair, always out of order,
And never going to be right, being a watch,

But being watch'd that it may still go right!
Nay, to be perjured, which is worst of all;
And, among three, to love the worst of all;
A wightly wanton with a velvet brow,
With two pitch-balls stuck in her face for eyes;
Ay, and by heaven, one that will do the deed
Though Argus were her eunuch and her guard:
And I to sigh for her! to watch for her!
To pray for her! Go to; it is a plague
That Cupid will impose for my neglect
Of his almighty dreadful little might.
Well, I will love, write, sigh, pray, sue and groan:
Some men must love my lady and some Joan.

Exit

Unless it is watched carefully to make sure it doesn't stray! No, to be guilty of breaking my oath, which is worst of all; And, out of three, to love the worst of all; A ghostly-pale, promiscuous woman with a velvet brow, With two pitch-black balls stuck in her face for eyes; Yes, and by heaven, one that will engage in intercourse Even if Argus, the beast with one hundred eyes were her eunuch and guard: And for me to sigh for her! To lose sleep over her! To pray for her! Go to; it is a plague That Cupid will impose on me for ignoring Of his almighty dreadful little power. Well I will love, write, sigh, pray, sue and groan: Some men must love women like my lady and some a virtuous woman like Joan of Arc.

ACT IV

SCENE I. The same.

Enter the PRINCESS, and her train, a Forester, BOYET, ROSALINE, MARIA, and KATHARINE

PRINCESS
Was that the king, that spurred his horse so hard
Against the steep uprising of the hill?

Was that the king that spurred his horse so hard Against the steep uprising of the hill?

BOYET
I know not; but I think it was not he.

I don't know; but I don't think it was him.

PRINCESS
Whoe'er a' was, a' show'd a mounting mind.
Well, lords, to-day we shall have our dispatch:
On Saturday we will return to France.
Then, forester, my friend, where is the bush
That we must stand and play the murderer in?

Whoever he was, it seemed like he had something pressing on his mind. Well, lords, today we will serve our purpose here: On Saturday we will return to France. So, forester, my friend, where is the bush That serves as the hunter's station where we will play the murderer in?

Forester
Hereby, upon the edge of yonder coppice;
A stand where you may make the fairest shoot.

Just there, upon the edge of that thicket; There's a station where you can make the fairest shot.

PRINCESS
I thank my beauty, I am fair that shoot,
And thereupon thou speak'st the fairest shoot.

Thanks to my beauty, I am the one shooting who is fairest, And that's why you call it the fairest shot.

Forester
Pardon me, madam, for I meant not so.

Pardon me, madam, I didn't mean it like that.

PRINCESS
What, what? first praise me and again say no?
O short-lived pride! Not fair? alack for woe!

What's that? First praise me and then take it back? O short-lived pride? I'm not beautiful? How sad that makes me!

Forester
Yes, madam, fair.

Yes, madam, you are beautiful.

PRINCESS
Nay, never paint me now:
Where fair is not, praise cannot mend the brow.
Here, good my glass, take this for telling true:
Fair payment for foul words is more than due.

No, don't flatter me now: Where there is no beauty, praise will not fix that face. Here, my true mirror, take this for telling me the truth: It's only fair to pay for foul but honest words.

Forester

Nothing but fair is that which you inherit.

PRINCESS
See see, my beauty will be saved by merit!
O heresy in fair, fit for these days!
A giving hand, though foul, shall have fair
praise.
But come, the bow: now mercy goes to kill,
And shooting well is then accounted ill.
Thus will I save my credit in the shoot:
Not wounding, pity would not let me do't;
If wounding, then it was to show my skill,
That more for praise than purpose meant to kill.
And out of question so it is sometimes,
Glory grows guilty of detested crimes,
When, for fame's sake, for praise, an outward
part,
We bend to that the working of the heart;
As I for praise alone now seek to spill
The poor deer's blood, that my heart means no
ill.

BOYET
Do not curst wives hold that self-sovereignty
Only for praise sake, when they strive to be
Lords o'er their lords?

PRINCESS
Only for praise: and praise we may afford
To any lady that subdues a lord.

BOYET
Here comes a member of the commonwealth.

Enter COSTARD

COSTARD
God dig-you-den all! Pray you, which is the
head lady?

PRINCESS
Thou shalt know her, fellow, by the rest that
have no heads.

COSTARD
Which is the greatest lady, the highest?

You are nothing but beautiful.

And see now, my beauty will be complimented after receiving payment! O heresy regarding beauty, fit for these days! A giving hand, though it be ugly will get praised as lovely. But come now, give me the bow and arrow: the princess goes in for the kill, And when a merciful person like a princess shoots well, they are considered ill. So I will save my reputation in the shot: If I miss I can say that it was pity that held me back: If I don't then it was to show my skill, I shot accurately more for praise than for the sake of killing. And undoubtedly, so it is sometimes, We become guilty of horrible crimes for the sake of glory, When, for the sake of fame, of praise, or some other superficial thing, We force out hearts to adapt to seeking fame; Just like I am now only for praise seeking to spill This poor deer's blood, that my heart wishes no harm.

Don't shrewish wives hold that self-sovereignty Only for the sake of praise, when they try to be Lords over their husbands?

Only for praise: we can afford to praise Any woman that can subdue a man.

Here comes a member of the ordinary citizenry.

God give you a good evening! Please, which one of you is the head lady?

You shall know her, fellow, by seeing that the rest have no heads.

Which is the greatest lady, the highest?

PRINCESS
The thickest and the tallest.

The thickest and the tallest.

COSTARD
The thickest and the tallest! it is so; truth is truth.
An your waist, mistress, were as slender as my wit,
One o' these maids' girdles for your waist should be fit.
Are not you the chief woman? you are the thickest here.

The thickest and the tallest! That is so; truth is truth.
And your waist, mistress, is as slender as my wit,
One of these maids' girdles should be fit to your waist.
Are you the chief woman? You are the thickest here.

PRINCESS
What's your will, sir? what's your will?

What do you need, sir? why are you here?

COSTARD
I have a letter from Monsieur Biron to one Lady Rosaline.

I have a letter from Monsieur Biron to one Lady Rosaline.

PRINCESS
O, thy letter, thy letter! he's a good friend of mine:
Stand aside, good bearer. Boyet, you can carve;
Break up this capon.

O, your letter, your letter! he's a good friend of mine:
Stand aside, good messenger. Boyet you can carve; Cut open this letter.

BOYET
I am bound to serve.
This letter is mistook, it importeth none here;
It is writ to Jaquenetta.

I am bound to serve.
This letter is misdirected, it concerns no one here; It is written to Jaquenetta.

PRINCESS
We will read it, I swear.
Break the neck of the wax, and every one give ear.

We will read it, I swear.
Break the wax seal and read it aloud.

Reads

BOYET
'By heaven, that thou art fair, is most infallible; true, that thou art beauteous; truth itself, that thou art lovely. More fairer than fair, beautiful than beauteous, truer than truth itself, have commiseration on thy heroical vassal! The magnanimous and most illustrate king Cophetua

'Heaven knows, that you are pretty, is completely certain; True, that you are beautiful; truth itself, that You are lovely. Prettier than pretty, more gorgeous Than beautiful, truer than truth itself, have Sympathy on your heroic liege! The Generous and most illustrious kind

set
eye upon the pernicious and indubitate beggar
Zenelophon; and he it was that might rightly
say,
Veni, vidi, vici; which to annothanize in the
vulgar,--O base and obscure vulgar!--videlicet,
He
came, saw, and overcame: he came, one; saw
two;
overcame, three. Who came? the king: why did
he
come? to see: why did he see? to overcome: to
whom came he? to the beggar: what saw he?
The
beggar: who overcame he? the beggar. The
conclusion is victory: on whose side? the king's.
The captive is enriched: on whose side? The
beggar's. The catastrophe is a nuptial: on whose
side? the king's: no, on both in one, or one in
both. I am the king; for so stands the
comparison:
thou the beggar; for so witnesseth thy lowliness.
Shall I command thy love? I may: shall I
enforce
thy love? I could: shall I entreat thy love? I
will. What shalt thou exchange for rags? robes;
for tittles? titles; for thyself? me. Thus,
expecting thy reply, I profane my lips on thy
foot,
my eyes on thy picture. and my heart on thy
every
part. Thine, in the dearest design of industry,

DON ADRIANO DE ARMADO.'
Thus dost thou hear the Nemean lion roar
'Gainst thee, thou lamb, that standest as his prey.
Submissive fall his princely feet before,
And he from forage will incline to play:
But if thou strive, poor soul, what art thou then?
Food for his rage, repasture for his den.

PRINCESS
What plume of feathers is he that indited this
letter?
What vane? what weathercock? did you ever
hear better?

Cophetua had
His eye set upon the baneful and undoubted
beggar Zenelophon; and it was he that could
rightly say,
Veni, vidi, vici; which to interpret in the
Vernacular, --O base and obscure vernacular!--
namely, He
Came, saw, and conquered: he came, one; saw,
two;
Conquered, three. Who came? The king; why
did he
Come? To see: why did he see? To conquer: to
Whom did he come? To the beggar: what did he
see? The
beggar: who did he conquer? The beggar. The
conclusion is victory: on whose side? The
king's. The captive is enriched: on whose side?
The Beggar's. The climax of the story is a
wedding: on whose Side? The king's; no, on
both in one, or one in Both. I am the king; that is
how the comparison stands:
You are the beggar; as you yourself are aware
of your lowliness.
Shall I command your love? I may: shall I
enforce Your love? I could: shall I entreat your
love? I Will. What will you exchange for rags?
Robes; For dots? Titles; for yourself? Me. So,
Expecting your reply, I desecrate my lips on
your foot,
My eyes on your picture, and my heart of every
Part of you. Yours, in the most excellent pattern
of zealous gallantry,

So do you hear the Nimean Lion roar
Against you, you lamb, that stand as his prey.
Fall submissively before his princely feet,
And he from ravening will incline to play:
But if you struggle, poor soul, what are you
then? Feeding for his rage, food for his den.

What kind of gaudy bird is the man that wrote
this letter?
What weather-vain, what weathercock? Have
you ever heard better?

BOYET
I am much deceived but I remember the style.

I am much deceived unless I remember the style.

PRINCESS
Else your memory is bad, going o'er it erewhile.

Or else your memory is bad, going over it just now.

BOYET
This Armado is a Spaniard, that keeps here in court;
A phantasime, a Monarcho, and one that makes sport
To the prince and his bookmates.

This Armado is a Spaniard, that live here in court;
He entertains fantastic notions, displays absurd pretentions, and entertains
The prince and his study-mates.

PRINCESS
Thou fellow, a word:
Who gave thee this letter?

You, fellow, a word:
Who gave you this letter?

COSTARD
I told you; my lord.

I told you; my lord.

PRINCESS
To whom shouldst thou give it?

You are you delivering it to?

COSTARD
From my lord to my lady.

From my lord to my lady.

PRINCESS
From which lord to which lady?

From which lord to which lady?

COSTARD
From my lord Biron, a good master of mine,
To a lady of France that he call'd Rosaline.

From my lord Biron, a good master of mine,
To a lady from France that he called Rosaline.

PRINCESS
Thou hast mistaken his letter. Come, lords, away.

You have mistaken his letter. Come, lords, let's go.

To ROSALINE
Here, sweet, put up this: 'twill be thine another day.

Here, my sweet, put this away: it will be your turn another day.

Exeunt PRINCESS and train

BOYET
Who is the suitor? who is the suitor?

Who is the archer? Who is the archer?

ROSALINE
Shall I teach you to know?

Shall I teach you to know?

BOYET
Ay, my continent of beauty.

Yes, my container of all beauty.

ROSALINE
Why, she that bears the bow.
Finely put off!

Why, she that holds to bow.
Finely answered!

BOYET
My lady goes to kill horns; but, if thou marry,
Hang me by the neck, if horns that year
miscarry.
Finely put on!

My lady goes to kill the horned deers; but if you
marry, Hang me by the neck, if there is not an
abundance of cuckold's horns that year.
Finely applied!

ROSALINE
Well, then, I am the shooter.

Well, then I am the shooter.

BOYET
And who is your deer?

And who is your dear one?

ROSALINE
If we choose by the horns, yourself come not
near.
Finely put on, indeed!

If we're choosing based on horns, you yourself
don't stand a chance.
Finely answered indeed!

MARIA
You still wrangle with her, Boyet, and she
strikes
at the brow.

You still wrangle with her, Boyet, and she takes
Good aim right between your eyes.

BOYET
But she herself is hit lower: have I hit her now?

But she herself is hit lower, in the heart: have I
hit her now?

ROSALINE
Shall I come upon thee with an old saying, that
was
a man when King Pepin of France was a little
boy, as
touching the hit it?

Shall I answer with an old saying, that was
Already old when King Pepin of France was a
little boy, sung
Bawdily while dancing?

BOYET
So I may answer thee with one as old, that was a
woman when Queen Guinover of Britain was a
little

I can answer you with one as old, that was
Aready old when Queen Guinevere of Britain
was a little

wench, as touching the hit it.

Girl, sung bawdily while dancing.

ROSALINE
'Thou canst not hit it, hit it, hit it,
Thou canst not hit it, my good man.'

'You cannot hit it, hit it, hit it,
You cannot hit it, my good man.'

BOYET
'An I cannot, cannot, cannot,
An I cannot, another can.'

'And I cannot, cannot, cannot,
And I cannot, another can.'

Exeunt ROSALINE and KATHARINE

COSTARD
By my troth, most pleasant: how both did fit it!

My goodness, that was very pleasant: how both
of them fit it!

MARIA
A mark marvellous well shot, for they both did
hit it.

A target marvelously well shot, since they both
hit it.

BOYET
A mark! O, mark but that mark! A mark, says
my lady!
Let the mark have a prick in't, to mete at, if it
may be.

A target! O, mark that target! A target says my
lady!
Let the mark have a bullseye in it, to aim at, if it
may be.

MARIA
Wide o' the bow hand! i' faith, your hand is out.

You missed the target to the left side, your hand
is inaccurate.

COSTARD
Indeed, a' must shoot nearer, or he'll ne'er hit the
clout.

Indeed, he must shoot nearer, or he'll never hit
the bullseye.

BOYET
An if my hand be out, then belike your hand is
in.

And If my hand is inaccurate, perhaps your
hand is not.

COSTARD
Then will she get the upshoot by cleaving the
pin.

Then she will get the best shot, by cleaving the
nail in two.

MARIA
Come, come, you talk greasily; your lips grow
foul.

Come, now, your talk is gross; your lips grow
foul.

COSTARD

She's too hard for you at pricks, sir: challenge her to bowl.

She's to hard for you at archery, sir: challenge her to bowl.

BOYET
I fear too much rubbing. Good night, my good owl.

I fear too much rubbing of the bowling balls. Goodnight, my good owl.

Exeunt BOYET and MARIA

COSTARD
By my soul, a swain! a most simple clown!
Lord, Lord, how the ladies and I have put him down!
O' my troth, most sweet jests! most incony vulgar wit!
When it comes so smoothly off, so obscenely, as it
were, so fit.
Armado o' th' one side,--O, a most dainty man!
To see him walk before a lady and to bear her fan!
To see him kiss his hand! and how most sweetly a'
will swear!
And his page o' t' other side, that handful of wit!
Ah, heavens, it is a most pathetical nit!
Sola, sola!

By my soul, a country boy! A simple clown!
Lord, lord how the ladies and I put him down just now!
Oh my word, such funny jokes! How rare and fine Vulgar wit!
When it comes so smoothly off, so obscenely, as it
Were, so fit.
Armado on the one side, -- Such a refined and dainty man! To see him walk in front of a lady and carry her fan!
To see him kiss his hand! And how most sweetly he
Will swear!
And his page on the otherside, that handful of wit! Oh heavens, he is a most touching little mite. To hunt, to hunt!

Shout within

Exit COSTARD, running

SCENE II. The same.

Enter HOLOFERNES, SIR NATHANIEL, and DULL

SIR NATHANIEL
Very reverend sport, truly; and done in the testimony
of a good conscience.

A very honorable sport, and done with a warrant
Of a good conscience.

HOLOFERNES
The deer was, as you know, sanguis, in blood; ripe
as the pomewater, who now hangeth like a jewel in
the ear of caelo, the sky, the welkin, the heaven;
and anon falleth like a crab on the face of terra,
the soil, the land, the earth.

The deer was, as you know, in prime condition; ripe
Like the pomewater apple, who now hangs like a jewel in
The ear of caelo, the sky, the welkin, the heaven;
And eventually falls like a crab apple on the face of terra, The soil, the land, the earth.

SIR NATHANIEL
Truly, Master Holofernes, the epithets are sweetly
varied, like a scholar at the least: but, sir, I
assure ye, it was a buck of the first head.

Truly, Master Holofernes, the epithets are sweetly
Varied, like a scholar to say the least: but, sir, I
Assure you, it was a buck of about five years, with newly full antlers.

HOLOFERNES
Sir Nathaniel, haud credo.

Sir Nathaniel, I don't believe it.

DULL
'Twas not a haud credo; 'twas a pricket.

Not it was not a haud credo; it was a young buck.

HOLOFERNES
Most barbarous intimation! yet a kind of
insinuation, as it were, in via, in way, of
explication; facere, as it were, replication, or
rather, ostentare, to show, as it were, his
inclination, after his undressed, unpolished,
uneducated, unpruned, untrained, or rather,
unlettered, or ratherest, unconfirmed fashion, to
insert again my haud credo for a deer.

What a barbaric interruption! Yet a kind of
Insinuation, as it were, in viw, in a way, of
Expounding; to make, as it were, explanation, or
Rather, ostentatiously, showing, as it were, his
Inclination, after his undressed, unpolished,
Uneducated, unpruned, untrained, or rather,
Unlettered, or unconfirmed way, to
interpret again my 'haud credo' to mean a deer.

DULL
I said the deer was not a haud credo; twas a pricket.

I said the deer was not a haud credo; it was a young buck.

HOLOFERNES

Twice-sod simplicity, his coctus!
O thou monster Ignorance, how deformed dost
thou look!

SIR NATHANIEL
Sir, he hath never fed of the dainties that are
bred
in a book; he hath not eat paper, as it were; he
hath not drunk ink: his intellect is not
replenished; he is only an animal, only sensible
in
the duller parts:
And such barren plants are set before us, that we
thankful should be,
Which we of taste and feeling are, for those
parts that
do fructify in us more than he.
For as it would ill become me to be vain,
indiscreet, or a fool,
So were there a patch set on learning, to see him
in a school:
But omne bene, say I; being of an old father's
mind,
Many can brook the weather that love not the
wind.

DULL
You two are book-men: can you tell me by your
wit
What was a month old at Cain's birth, that's not
five
weeks old as yet?

HOLOFERNES
Dictynna, goodman Dull; Dictynna, goodman
Dull.

DULL
What is Dictynna?

SIR NATHANIEL
A title to Phoebe, to Luna, to the moon.

HOLOFERNES
The moon was a month old when Adam was no
more,

Twice boiled simplicity, twice cooked!
O you monster, Ignorance, how deformed you
look!

Sir he has never fed from the foods that are bred
In a book; he has not eaten paper, as it were; he
Has not drunk ink: his intellect is not
Replenished; he is only an animal, only capable
of perception in
The duller parts:
And just like the barren plants that are set
before us, that we
Should be thankful for.
We who have taste and feeling are, for those
parts that
Do grow fruitful in us more than in him.
Just as it would not be becoming for me to be
vain, indiscreet or a fool,
It would be the same to set a dolt or fool to start
learning:
But I say all is well; being of the opinion of an
ancient sage,
Many can put up with the weather that do not
love the wind.

You two are smart men: can you tell me by your
wit
What was a month old when Cain was born, but
that's not five
Weeks old as of yet?

Dictynna, my good man Dull; Dictynna, my
good man.

What is Dictynna?

Another name for Phoebe, Luna, for the moon.

The moon was a month old when Adam was no
more,

And raught not to five weeks when he came to five-score.
The allusion holds in the exchange.

And hadn't reached five weeks when he became Fifty years old.
The riddle remains valid in the substitution of Adam for Cain.

DULL
'Tis true indeed; the collusion holds in the exchange.

It's true indeed; the conspiracy stays in the exchange.

HOLOFERNES
God comfort thy capacity! I say, the allusion holds
in the exchange.

God comfort your tiny brain! I said, the riddle still applies
If you exchange the names.

DULL
And I say, the pollution holds in the exchange; for
the moon is never but a month old: and I say beside
that, 'twas a pricket that the princess killed.

And I say, the pollution stays in the exchange; for
The moon is never more than a month old: and I say besides
That, it was a young buck that the princess killed.

HOLOFERNES
Sir Nathaniel, will you hear an extemporal epitaph
on the death of the deer? And, to humour the ignorant, call I the deer the princess killed a pricket.

Sir Nathaniel, will you hear an improvised epitaph
On the death of the deer? And, to humor the Ignorant one, I'll call the deer the princess killed a young buck.

SIR NATHANIEL
Perge, good Master Holofernes, perge; so it shall
please you to abrogate scurrility.

Proceed, good Master Holofernes, proceed; so it will
Please you to refrain from any obscene abuse.

HOLOFERNES
I will something affect the letter, for it argues facility.
The preyful princess pierced and prick'd a pretty pleasing pricket;
Some say a sore; but not a sore, till now made sore with shooting.
The dogs did yell: put L to sore, then sorel jumps
from thicket;
Or pricket sore, or else sorel; the people fall a-hooting.
If sore be sore, then L to sore makes fifty sores

I will somewhat make use of alliteration, for it requires skill.
The princess intent upon a prey, pierced and shot a pretty Pleasing young buck;
Some say a sore, a deer of four years; but it was not a sore, until just now Made sore with being shot. The dogs yelled; put fifty to sore, then sorel, a dear of three years, jumps
From the thicket
Either a young buck of four years, or else three; the people start hooting.
If sore is sore, the fifty to sore makes fifty sores

one sorel.
Of one sore I an hundred make by adding but one more L.

One sorel.
I can make one sore into a hundred by adding one more fifty.

SIR NATHANIEL
A rare talent!

A rare talent!

DULL
[**Aside**] If a talent be a claw, look how he claws him with a talent.

[Aside] If a talent were a claw, look how he flatters Him with his talons.

HOLOFERNES
This is a gift that I have, simple, simple; a foolish extravagant spirit, full of forms, figures, shapes, objects, ideas, apprehensions, motions, revolutions: these are begot in the ventricle of memory, nourished in the womb of pia mater, and
delivered upon the mellowing of occasion. But the
gift is good in those in whom it is acute, and I am
thankful for it.

This is a gift that I have, simple, simple; a Foolish extravagant spirit, full of forms, figures, Shapes, objects, ideas, apprehensions, motions, Revolutions: these come from the part of the brain used for Memory, nourished in the womb of the membrane surrounding the brain, and Is delivered when the moment is ripe. But the Gift is good for those people that have it acutely, and I am Thankful for it.

SIR NATHANIEL
Sir, I praise the Lord for you; and so may my parishioners; for their sons are well tutored by you, and their daughters profit very greatly under
you: you are a good member of the commonwealth.

Sir, I praise the Lord for you; and so are the people in my parish; for their sons are well tutored by you, and their daughters profit very greatly under Your teaching: you are a good member of the community.

HOLOFERNES
Mehercle, if their sons be ingenuous, they shall want no instruction; if their daughters be capable,
I will put it to them: but vir sapit qui pauca loquitur; a soul feminine saluteth us.

By Hercules, if their sons are naïve they will Not Lack instruction; I their daughters are capable, I will put it to them: but he is a wise man who Speaks little; a feminine soul is saluting us.

Enter JAQUENETTA and COSTARD

JAQUENETTA
God give you good morrow, master Parson.

God give you a good day, master Parson.

HOLOFERNES
Master Parson, quasi pers-on. An if one should

Master Parson, you mean person. And if one

be
pierced, which is the one?

should be
The pierced-one, which is the one?

COSTARD
Marry, master schoolmaster, he that is likest to a
hogshead.

Well, master schoolteacher, he that is the most
alike to a hogshead.

HOLOFERNES
Piercing a hogshead! a good lustre of conceit in
a
tuft of earth; fire enough for a flint, pearl enough
for a swine: 'tis pretty; it is well.

Getting drunk! A good spark of fancy in a
tuft of earth; enough fire for a flint, enough
pearl
For a swine: it's pretty, it is good.

JAQUENETTA
Good master Parson, be so good as read me this
letter: it was given me by Costard, and sent me
from Don Armado: I beseech you, read it.

Good master Person, if you would be so good as
to read me this
Letter: it was given to me by Costard, and sent
to me From Don Armado: I beg you, read it.

HOLOFERNES
Fauste, precor gelida quando pecus omne sub
umbra
Ruminat,--and so forth. Ah, good old Mantuan!
I
may speak of thee as the traveller doth of
Venice;
Venetia, Venetia,
Chi non ti vede non ti pretia.
Old Mantuan, old Mantuan! who understandeth
thee
not, loves thee not. Ut, re, sol, la, mi, fa.
Under pardon, sir, what are the contents? or
rather,
as Horace says in his--What, my soul, verses?

Faustus, I beg, while all the cattle chew their
cud
In the cool shade—and so forth. Ah good old
Mantuan! I
Could talk about you the way a traveler talks of
Venice;
Venice, Venice,
He who sees you not, loves you not.
Old Manuan, old Mantuan! Who understands
you
Not, loves you not. Do, re, mi, fa so , la, ti, do.
I beg pardon, sir, what are the contents of this
letter? or rather,
As Horace says in his—What, my soul, verses?

SIR NATHANIEL
Ay, sir, and very learned.

Yes, sir, and very educated.

HOLOFERNES
Let me hear a staff, a stanze, a verse; lege,
domine.

Let me hear a staff, a stanza, a verse; read,
master.

SIR NATHANIEL
[Reads]
If love make me forsworn, how shall I swear to
love?

If love makes me break my oath, how can I
swear to love?

Ah, never faith could hold, if not to beauty
vow'd!
Though to myself forsworn, to thee I'll faithful
prove:
Those thoughts to me were oaks, to thee like
osiers bow'd.
Study his bias leaves and makes his book thine
eyes,
Where all those pleasures live that art would
comprehend:
If knowledge be the mark, to know thee shall
suffice;
Well learned is that tongue that well can thee
commend,
All ignorant that soul that sees thee without
wonder;
Which is to me some praise that I thy parts
admire:
Thy eye Jove's lightning bears, thy voice his
dreadful thunder,
Which not to anger bent, is music and sweet
fire.
Celestial as thou art, O, pardon, love, this
wrong,
That sings heaven's praise with such an earthly
tongue.

HOLOFERNES
You find not the apostraphas, and so miss the
accent: let me supervise the canzonet. Here are
only numbers ratified; but, for the elegancy,
facility, and golden cadence of poesy, caret.
Ovidius Naso was the man: and why, indeed,
Naso,
but for smelling out the odouriferous flowers of
fancy, the jerks of invention? Imitari is nothing:
so doth the hound his master, the ape his keeper,
the tired horse his rider. But, damosella virgin,
was this directed to you?

JAQUENETTA
Ay, sir, from one Monsieur Biron, one of the
strange
queen's lords.

HOLOFERNES

*Oh, faith could never hold, if it is not vowed to
beauty!*
*Though I have broken my promise to myself, I'll
prove to be faithful to you;*
*Those thoughts that were like strong oak trees,
that have bowed like Willow branches.*
*Study leaves his normal inclination, and makes
his book your eyes,*
*Where all the pleasures live that art would
Understand:*
*If knowledge is the goal, to know you will
suffice;*
*I know very well the language that can praise
you,*
*Anyone who looks at you without wonder is
ignorant;*
Which in a way praises me for admiring you:
*In your eyes, Zeus' lightning, in your voice, his
dreadful thunder,*
*Which is not full of anger, it's full of music and
sweet fire.*
*Celestial as you are, O, pardon me love, for this
wrong,*
*That tries to sing heaven's praise with such an
earthly tongue.*

*You didn't see the apostrophes, so you missed
the Accent: let me glance over the poem. Here
the language is Merely made metrical; but as
for elegance, usefulness and golden cadence of
poetry, it's lacking. Ovidius Naso was the man.
And indeed he was Nasal
In order to smell the odorous flowers of
Fantasy, the stroke of imagination? To imitate is
nothing: As the hound does what his master
commands, the ape obeys his keeper the tired
horse obeys his rider. But, girl was this meant
for you?*

*Yes, sir, from Monsier Biron, one of the foreign
Queen's lords.*

I will overglance the superscript: 'To the snow-white hand of the most beauteous Lady Rosaline.' I will look again on the intellect of the letter, for the nomination of the party writing to the person written unto: 'Your ladyship's in all desired employment, BIRON.' Sir Nathaniel, this
Biron is one of the votaries with the king; and here
he hath framed a letter to a sequent of the stranger
queen's, which accidentally, or by the way of progression, hath miscarried. Trip and go, my sweet; deliver this paper into the royal hand of the
king: it may concern much. Stay not thy compliment; I forgive thy duty; adieu.

I will take a look at the address: 'To the snow-white hand of the most beautiful Lady Rosaline.' I will look again at the meaning of The letter, for the naming of the person writing to the person written to: 'Your ladyship's much desired service, Biron.' Sir Nathaniel, this Biron is one of the king's party; and here he has written a letter to the attendant of the foreign queen's, which accidentally, or by process of delivery, was delivered to the wrong person. Hurry and go, my sweet; get this letter to the royal hand of the king: it may be important. Don't worry about Ceremony; No need to curtsy; Goodbye.

JAQUENETTA
Good Costard, go with me. Sir, God save your life!

Good Costard, go with me. Sir, God will grace you for it!

COSTARD
Have with thee, my girl.

I'll go with you, my girl.

Exeunt COSTARD and JAQUENETTA

SIR NATHANIEL
Sir, you have done this in the fear of God, very religiously; and, as a certain father saith,--

Sir, you have done this with respect of God, very Religiously; and, as a certain priest has said, --

HOLOFERNES
Sir tell me not of the father; I do fear colourable colours. But to return to the verses: did they please you, Sir Nathaniel?

Sir please do not speak of the priest; I do fear plausible Reasons. But to return to the letter: Did they please you, Sir Nathaniel?

SIR NATHANIEL
Marvellous well for the pen.

Marvellous penmanship.

HOLOFERNES
I do dine to-day at the father's of a certain pupil of mine; where, if, before repast, it shall please you to gratify the table with a grace, I will, on my
privilege I have with the parents of the foresaid

I will have dinner today at the house of the father of a certain student Of mine; where, if before feasting, it would please You to grace the table with a prayer, I will Have with the parents of the aforementioned

child or pupil, undertake your ben venuto; where I
will prove those verses to be very unlearned,
neither savouring of poetry, wit, nor invention: I
beseech your society.

child or student, ask for your welcome; where I
will prove those verses to be very dull,
and not poetic, witty, or imaginative: I
Ask for your company.

SIR NATHANIEL
And thank you too; for society, saith the text, is
the happiness of life.

And thank you too; for company, says the bible,
is What makes life happy.

HOLOFERNES
And, certes, the text most infallibly concludes it.

And, certainly, the text most reliably affirms it.

To DULL
Sir, I do invite you too; you shall not
say me nay: pauca verba. Away! the gentles are at
their game, and we will to our recreation.

Sir, I invite you too; you will not
tell me no: Few words. Come on! The gentlefolk
are at
Their game, and we will entertain ourselves as
well.

Exeunt

SCENE III. The same.

Enter BIRON, with a paper

BIRON
The king he is hunting the deer; I am coursing
myself: they have pitched a toil; I am toiling in
a pitch,--pitch that defiles: defile! a foul
word. Well, set thee down, sorrow! for so they
say
the fool said, and so say I, and I the fool: well
proved, wit! By the Lord, this love is as mad as
Ajax: it kills sheep; it kills me, I a sheep:
well proved again o' my side! I will not love: if
I do, hang me; i' faith, I will not. O, but her
eye,--by this light, but for her eye, I would not
love her; yes, for her two eyes. Well, I do
nothing
in the world but lie, and lie in my throat. By
heaven, I do love: and it hath taught me to
rhyme
and to be melancholy; and here is part of my
rhyme,
sonnets already: the clown bore it, the fool sent
it, and the lady hath it: sweet clown, sweeter
fool, sweetest lady! By the world, I would not
care
a pin, if the other three were in. Here comes one
with a paper: God give him grace to groan!

*The king is out hunting deer; I am pursuing
myself: they have set a trap; I am trapped
in Rosaline's eyes,-- the trap that defiles: defile!
An awful word. Well, sit down with me, sorrow!
For so they say
the fool says, and I say as well, so I must be a
fool: well proved, wit! By Lord, this love is as
mad as Ajax: it kills sheep; it kills me, so I must
be a sheep: well proved again for my credit! I
will not love: if I do, hang me; I promise, I will
not. O, but her Eye,--in this light, if not for her
eye, I would not love her; yes, for both her eyes.
Well, I do nothing
in the world but lie, and lie through my teeth.
By
heaven, I do love: and it has taught me to write
rhymes
and feel melancholy; and here is part of my
poem, sonnets already: the clown delivered it,
the fool sent it, and the lady has it: sweet clown,
sweeter fool, sweetest lady! By the world, I
would not care
at all, if the other three were involved. Here
comes one
With a letter: God give him grace to groan!*

Stands aside

Enter FERDINAND, with a paper

FERDINAND
Ay me!

Oh me!

BIRON
[Aside] Shot, by heaven! Proceed, sweet Cupid:
thou hast thumped him with thy bird-bolt under
the
left pap. In faith, secrets!

*Shot, by heaven! Come on, sweet Cupid:
you have hit him with your arrow under the
Left breast. He thinks he's alone, so he will tell
secrets!*

FERDINAND
[Reads]

So sweet a kiss the golden sun gives not
To those fresh morning drops upon the rose,
As thy eye-beams, when their fresh rays have
smote
The night of dew that on my cheeks down
flows:
Nor shines the silver moon one half so bright
Through the transparent bosom of the deep,
As doth thy face through tears of mine give
light;
Thou shinest in every tear that I do weep:
No drop but as a coach doth carry thee;
So ridest thou triumphing in my woe.
Do but behold the tears that swell in me,
And they thy glory through my grief will show:
But do not love thyself; then thou wilt keep
My tears for glasses, and still make me weep.
O queen of queens! how far dost thou excel,
No thought can think, nor tongue of mortal tell.
How shall she know my griefs? I'll drop the
paper:
Sweet leaves, shade folly. Who is he comes
here?

Steps aside

What, Longaville! and reading! listen, ear.

BIRON
Now, in thy likeness, one more fool appear!

Enter LONGAVILLE, with a paper

LONGAVILLE
Ay me, I am forsworn!

BIRON
Why, he comes in like a perjure, wearing
papers.

FERDINAND
In love, I hope: sweet fellowship in shame!

BIRON
One drunkard loves another of the name.

So sweet a kiss the golden sun cannot give
To the fresh dew drops on the rose,
As my eye-beams, when their fresh rays have
seen
The tears that flow nightly down my cheeks:
Nor does the silver moon shine half as bright
through the transparent bosom of the ocean,
As does my face through my tears which give
light;
You shine in every tear I weep
Not as a drop, but like a carriage they carry you
So you ride, taking triumph in my woe.
Do notice the tears that swell in me,
And they will show your glory through my grief:
But do not love yourself; then you will keep
my tears for mirrors, and still cause me to cry.
O queen of queens! How excellent you are,
No thought can think, nor mortal tongue can tell
How can she know my grief? I'll drop the
letter:
Sweet leaves, hide my foolishness. Who is that
coming here?

What, Longaville! And reading! Let's listen
closely.

Now, just like you, another fool will appear!

Oh me, I have broken my oath!

Why, he acts like he has told a lie under oath,
wearing that letter.

In love, I hope: we are companions in our
shame!

One drunkard loves another drunkard.

LONGAVILLE

Am I the first that have been perjured so?

Am I the first that has lied so?

BIRON

I could put thee in comfort. Not by two that I know:
Thou makest the triumviry, the corner-cap of society,
The shape of Love's Tyburn that hangs up simplicity.

I could comfort you. I already know of two:
You make it a triumvirate, a third corner for our
three corner cap of company,
The shape of Love's execution chamber that
hangs the simple.

LONGAVILLE

I fear these stubborn lines lack power to move:
O sweet Maria, empress of my love!
These numbers will I tear, and write in prose.

I'm afraid these difficult lines lack the power to
persuade: O sweet Maria, Queen of my love!
These verses I'll shred and re-write in prose.

BIRON

O, rhymes are guards on wanton Cupid's hose:
Disfigure not his slop.

O, rhymes are embroideries on promiscuous
Cupid's pants Don't disfigure his codpiece.

LONGAVILLE

This same shall go.
Reads
Did not the heavenly rhetoric of thine eye,
'Gainst whom the world cannot hold argument,
Persuade my heart to this false perjury?
Vows for thee broke deserve not punishment.
A woman I forswore; but I will prove,
Thou being a goddess, I forswore not thee:
My vow was earthly, thou a heavenly love;
Thy grace being gain'd cures all disgrace in me.
Vows are but breath, and breath a vapour is:
Then thou, fair sun, which on my earth dost shine,
Exhalest this vapour-vow; in thee it is:
If broken then, it is no fault of mine:
If by me broke, what fool is not so wise
To lose an oath to win a paradise?

This will go as follows:

Did not the heavenly way you spoke with your
eyes Against whom the whole world cannot find
fault Persuade me to commit this perjury
The vows I broke for you cannot be punished
A woman I committed to; but I will prove,
That since you are a goddess, I didn't commit to
you My vow was of the earth, by you are from
the heavens Gaining your approval cures all of
my disgrace Vows are spoken with breath, and
breath is just air: Then you, a fair sun, on my
earth do shine,
Exhales this air-vow; in you it is:
If broken, it's not my fault.
If I break it, what fool is not wise enough
As to break an oath in order to win paradise?

BIRON

This is the liver-vein, which makes flesh a deity,
A green goose a goddess: pure, pure idolatry.
God amend us, God amend! we are much out o'
the way.

This is the style of a lover, which turns flesh into
a God, A young girl into a goddess: pure, pure
idolatry.

LONGAVILLE
By whom shall I send this?--Company! stay.

But who will deliver this?— All of you! Wait.

Steps aside

BIRON
All hid, all hid; an old infant play.
Like a demigod here sit I in the sky.
And wretched fools' secrets heedfully o'ereye.
More sacks to the mill! O heavens, I have my
wish!

*He didn't see me, he didn't see me; a game of
hide n' seek Like a god here I sit elevated above
all. And these wretched fools' secrets I
overheard. There's more to come! O heavens,
my wish was granted!*

Enter DUMAIN, with a paper

Dumain transform'd! four woodcocks in a dish!

*Dumain is transformed! We're four dumb birds
in a dish!*

DUMAIN
O most divine Kate!

O most divine Kate!

BIRON
O most profane coxcomb!

O most profane conceited man!

DUMAIN
By heaven, the wonder in a mortal eye!

By heaven, the wonder in her human eye!

BIRON
By earth, she is not, corporal, there you lie.

*By earth, she's not wonderful, officer, that's a
lie.*

DUMAIN
Her amber hair for foul hath amber quoted.

Her amber hair makes real amber seem ugly.

BIRON
An amber-colour'd raven was well noted.

*And so, a raven was described as amber-
colored.*

DUMAIN
As upright as the cedar.

As upright as a cedar tree.

BIRON
Stoop, I say;
Her shoulder is with child.

*I say she stoops;
Her shoulder looks like it's pregnant.*

DUMAIN
As fair as day.

As pale and bright as daylight.

BIRON
Ay, as some days; but then no sun must shine.

Sure, on some days; when the sun doesn't shine.

DUMAIN
O that I had my wish!

O that my wish could be granted!

LONGAVILLE
And I had mine!

And mine too!

FERDINAND
And I mine too, good Lord!

And mine too, good Lord!

BIRON
Amen, so I had mine: is not that a good word?

Amen, so I mine as well: isn't that nice of me?

DUMAIN
I would forget her; but a fever she
Reigns in my blood and will remember'd be.

*I would forget her; but she heats
My blood up so much I can't forget it.*

BIRON
A fever in your blood! why, then incision
Would let her out in saucers: sweet misprision!

Heats your blood! Why, if we cut you

DUMAIN
Once more I'll read the ode that I have writ.

I'll read the ode I wrote again.

BIRON
Once more I'll mark how love can vary wit.

*Once more I'll see how love has nothing to do
with intelligence.*

DUMAIN
[Reads]
On a day--alack the day!--
Love, whose month is ever May,
Spied a blossom passing fair
Playing in the wanton air:
Through the velvet leaves the wind,
All unseen, can passage find;
That the lover, sick to death,
Wish himself the heaven's breath.
Air, quoth he, thy cheeks may blow;
Air, would I might triumph so!
But, alack, my hand is sworn
Ne'er to pluck thee from thy thorn;
Vow, alack, for youth unmeet,
Youth so apt to pluck a sweet!
Do not call it sin in me,
That I am forsworn for thee;
Thou for whom Jove would swear

*On a day—oh that day!--
Love, whose prime month is always May,
Saw a pretty flower in passing
Playing in the promiscuous air:
Through the velvety leaves the wind,
though not seen, can find a way
So that the lover, deathly ill
wishes for himself a breath from heaven.
'Air' he said, 'blow your cheeks'
'Air, so that I could triumph!'
But, oh no, I swore
To never pluck you from your stem;
I promise, oh, for a virgin youth,
A youth so likely to grab something sweet!
Do not call it a sin,
That I have committed to you;
You, who Jove would swear*

Juno but an Ethiope were;
And deny himself for Jove,
Turning mortal for thy love.
This will I send, and something else more plain,
That shall express my true love's fasting pain.
O, would the king, Biron, and Longaville,
Were lovers too! Ill, to example ill,
Would from my forehead wipe a perjured note;
For none offend where all alike do dote.

LONGAVILLE
[Advancing] Dumain, thy love is far from charity.
You may look pale, but I should blush, I know,
To be o'erheard and taken napping so.

FERDINAND
[Advancing] Come, sir, you blush; as his your case is such;
You chide at him, offending twice as much;
You do not love Maria; Longaville
Did never sonnet for her sake compile,
Nor never lay his wreathed arms athwart
His loving bosom to keep down his heart.
I have been closely shrouded in this bush
And mark'd you both and for you both did blush:
I heard your guilty rhymes, observed your fashion,
Saw sighs reek from you, noted well your passion:
Ay me! says one; O Jove! the other cries;
One, her hairs were gold, crystal the other's eyes:

To LONGAVILLE
You would for paradise break faith, and troth;

To DUMAIN
And Jove, for your love, would infringe an oath.
What will Biron say when that he shall hear
Faith so infringed, which such zeal did swear?
How will he scorn! how will he spend his wit!
How will he triumph, leap and laugh at it!
For all the wealth that ever I did see,
I would not have him know so much by me.

Juno was only an Ethiopian;
And would deny himself his pleasures, for Zeus
Would turn human for your love.
I'll send this, along with something else more
ordinary, That shall express the pain of my
hungering for my true love. O, if only the king,
Biron, and Longaville, Were lovers as well!
Sick, to be an example to the sick, Would help
me clear my mind of this oath-breaking; For you
can't offend when everyone's in love.

Dumain, your love is far from Christian love.
You look pale, but I should blush as well, I know
Since I was overheard and my private affairs
brought into the open, too.

Come on, sir, you blush; since your case is like
his;
You lecture him, when you're twice as offensive
You do not love Maria; Longaville
You never wrote a sonnet for her,
Nor did you ever fold your arms in sadness
Across your chest to keep your heart calm.
I have been hiding in this bush
And heard you both and for you both, I blushed:
I heard your sinful rhymes, and saw how you
acted,
Saw you sigh, was made aware of your passion:
Oh me! Says one; Oh God! cries the other;
One, says her hair is gold, the other says her
eyes are crystal blue:

You would break your faith for your paradise,
and truth;

And Zeus, for your love, would break a promise.
What will Biron say when he hears
Your faith so compromised, with how much
enthusiasm did he promise? How contemptuous
he will be! How he will go to his wit's end to
make fun! How he will triumph, leap and laugh
at it! Even for all the money in the world,

BIRON

Now step I forth to whip hypocrisy.

Advancing

Ah, good my liege, I pray thee, pardon me!
Good heart, what grace hast thou, thus to reprove
These worms for loving, that art most in love?
Your eyes do make no coaches; in your tears
There is no certain princess that appears;
You'll not be perjured, 'tis a hateful thing;
Tush, none but minstrels like of sonneting!
But are you not ashamed? nay, are you not,
All three of you, to be thus much o'ershot?
You found his mote; the king your mote did see;
But I a beam do find in each of three.
O, what a scene of foolery have I seen,
Of sighs, of groans, of sorrow and of teen!
O me, with what strict patience have I sat,
To see a king transformed to a gnat!
To see great Hercules whipping a gig,
And profound Solomon to tune a jig,
And Nestor play at push-pin with the boys,
And critic Timon laugh at idle toys!
Where lies thy grief, O, tell me, good Dumain?
And gentle Longaville, where lies thy pain?
And where my liege's? all about the breast:
A caudle, ho!

FERDINAND

Too bitter is thy jest.
Are we betray'd thus to thy over-view?

BIRON

Not you to me, but I betray'd by you:
I, that am honest; I, that hold it sin
To break the vow I am engaged in;
I am betray'd, by keeping company
With men like men of inconstancy.
When shall you see me write a thing in rhyme?
Or groan for love? or spend a minute's time
In pruning me? When shall you hear that I
Will praise a hand, a foot, a face, an eye,
A gait, a state, a brow, a breast, a waist,

I would want him to know so much about me.

Now I step forward to punish his hypocrisy.

Ah, my good liege, please excuse me!
Good heart, what grace do you have, to scold
These worms for loving, that are so love?
Your eyes make no coaches; in your tears
There is no certain princess that appears;
You won't be accused of oath-breaking, that
would be a hateful thing;
And no one but minstrels like writing sonnets!
But aren't you ashamed? No, aren't you
all three of you ashamed, to be so much in
error? You found his weakness; the king saw
yours; But I have found the defect in all three of
you. Oh, what a ridiculous scene I have
witnessed, Of sighs, of groans, of sorrow and of
affliction! Oh me, I sat there with such strict
patience To see a king transformed into a gnat!
To see great Hercules spinning a top,
And profound Solomon to play a jig
And Nestor play a child's game with the boys,
And the critic Timon to take delight in mindless
entertainments! Where is your grief, O tell me,
good Dumain? And gentle Longaville, where is
your pain? And where is my liege's? all over the
chest: These heartsick men could use some hot
ale!

Your jokes are too bitter.
Are we so betrayed by you over hearing?

Not you to me, but I've been betrayed by you:
I who am honest; I who took accountability for
my sin
To break the vow that I am engaged in;
I am betrayed by keeping company
With unfaithful men.
When will you see me write a thing in rhyme?
Or groan for love? Or spend a minute's time
In getting myself all dressed to impress? When
will you hear that I Will praise a hand, a foot,

80

A leg, a limb?

a face, an eye, A walk, an attitude, a brow, a breast, a waist A leg, a limb?

FERDINAND
Soft! whither away so fast?
A true man or a thief that gallops so?

*Stop! Where are you going so fast?
Only a thief runs away like that.*

BIRON
I post from love: good lover, let me go.

I hasten from love: good lover, let me go

Enter JAQUENETTA and COSTARD

JAQUENETTA
God bless the king!

God bless the king!

FERDINAND
What present hast thou there?

What present do you have there?

COSTARD
Some certain treason.

Some certain treason.

FERDINAND
What makes treason here?

What does treason have to do with us here?

COSTARD
Nay, it makes nothing, sir.

Nothing, sir.

FERDINAND
If it mar nothing neither,
The treason and you go in peace away together.

*If it's nothing then
The treason and you can go away in peace together.*

JAQUENETTA
I beseech your grace, let this letter be read:
Our parson misdoubts it; 'twas treason, he said.

*I ask your grace, please read this letter:
Our person suspects it; he said it was treason.*

FERDINAND
Biron, read it over.

Biron, read it aloud.

Giving him the paper
Where hadst thou it?

Where did you get it?

JAQUENETTA
Of Costard.

From Costard.

FERDINAND
Where hadst thou it?

And where did you get it?

COSTARD
Of Dun Adramadio, Dun Adramadio.

From Dun Adramadio, Dun Adramadio.

BIRON tears the letter

FERDINAND
How now! what is in you? why dost thou tear it?

What's this! what's come over you? Why did you tear it?

BIRON
A toy, my liege, a toy: your grace needs not fear it.

It's a toy, my liege, a toy: your grace does not need to fear it.

LONGAVILLE
It did move him to passion, and therefore let's hear it.

It moved him to a passion, so now he have to hear it.

DUMAIN
It is Biron's writing, and here is his name.

It's Biron's writing! And here is his name.

Gathering up the pieces

BIRON
[To COSTARD] Ah, you whoreson loggerhead! you were
born to do me shame.
Guilty, my lord, guilty! I confess, I confess.

[To COSTARD] Oh, you blockheaded son of a bitch! You were
Born just so that you could shame me.
Guilty, my lord, guilty! I confess, I confess.

FERDINAND
What?

What?

BIRON
That you three fools lack'd me fool to make up the mess:
He, he, and you, and you, my liege, and I,
Are pick-purses in love, and we deserve to die.
O, dismiss this audience, and I shall tell you more.

That you three fools only lack this fool, to make four fools.
He, he, and you and you, my liege and I,
Are thieves in love, and we deserve to die.
O, dismiss this audience, and I'll tell you the rest.

DUMAIN
Now the number is even.

Now the number is even.

BIRON
True, true; we are four.
Will these turtles be gone?

True, true; we are four.
Can these turtle dove lovers leave now?

FERDINAND

Hence, sirs; away!

Go, you two; Go on!

COSTARD

Walk aside the true folk, and let the traitors stay.

Let the true folk leave and the traitors stay.

Exeunt COSTARD and JAQUENETTA

BIRON

Sweet lords, sweet lovers, O, let us embrace!
As true we are as flesh and blood can be:
The sea will ebb and flow, heaven show his face;
Young blood doth not obey an old decree:
We cannot cross the cause why we were born;
Therefore of all hands must we be forsworn.

Sweet lords, sweet lovers, O, let us embrace each other! We are as true as flesh and blood can be: The sea will ebb and flow, heaven will show his face; Young blood does not obey an old decree: We cannot continue to defy love, the reason we were born; So we must inevitably break our vows.

FERDINAND

What, did these rent lines show some love of thine?

What, did these torn verses show some love of yours?

BIRON

Did they, quoth you? Who sees the heavenly Rosaline,
That, like a rude and savage man of Inde,
At the first opening of the gorgeous east,
Bows not his vassal head and strucken blind
Kisses the base ground with obedient breast?
What peremptory eagle-sighted eye
Dares look upon the heaven of her brow,
That is not blinded by her majesty?

*Did they, you ask? Who sees the heavenly Rosaline,
That, like a rude and savage man from India,
At the first dawning of the gorgeous east,
Does not bow his subordinate head and stricken blind Kiss the lowly ground with his obedient chest? What bold eye, keen as an eagle,
Dares look upon the heaven of her brow,
That is not blinded by her majesty?*

FERDINAND

What zeal, what fury hath inspired thee now?
My love, her mistress, is a gracious moon;
She an attending star, scarce seen a light.

What crazy madness has gotten a hold of you now? My love, her mistress, is a gracious moon; She is just a star attending to her, a light that can scarcely be seen.

BIRON

My eyes are then no eyes, nor I Biron:
O, but for my love, day would turn to night!
Of all complexions the cull'd sovereignty
Do meet, as at a fair, in her fair cheek,
Where several worthies make one dignity,
Where nothing wants that want itself doth seek.
Lend me the flourish of all gentle tongues,--
Fie, painted rhetoric! O, she needs it not:

*Then my eyes are not eyes, and I am not Biron:
O, without my love, day would turn to night!
Of all complexions that are deemed most worthy They meet, like at a fair, in her beautiful cheek,
Where several excellences make on supreme example of beauty, Where nothing lacks that desires itself seeks. Lend me the eloquence of all noble tongues,-- Ugh! Artificial rhetoric! O, she*

To things of sale a seller's praise belongs,
She passes praise; then praise too short doth blot.
A wither'd hermit, five-score winters worn,
Might shake off fifty, looking in her eye:
Beauty doth varnish age, as if new-born,
And gives the crutch the cradle's infancy:
O, 'tis the sun that maketh all things shine.

doesn't need that: A seller's praise belongs to things for sale, She is above praise; any praise of her is inadequate and detracts from her beauty. And hermit, withered by five years of winter, Might shed fifty years by looking in her eye: Beauty polishes age, as if new-born And give the crutch the infancy of a cradle: It is the sun that makes all things shine.

FERDINAND
By heaven, thy love is black as ebony.

By heaven, your love is black as ebony.

BIRON
Is ebony like her? O wood divine!
A wife of such wood were felicity.
O, who can give an oath? where is a book?
That I may swear beauty doth beauty lack,
If that she learn not of her eye to look:
No face is fair that is not full so black.

Is ebony liker her? O divine wood! A wife of that wood would be pure happiness. O, who here can swear me to an oath? Is there a bible around? So that I can swear that beauty isn't beauty at all Unless she learns what beauty is by looking at Rosaline: No face is pretty that isn't so fully black.

FERDINAND
O paradox! Black is the badge of hell,
The hue of dungeons and the suit of night;
And beauty's crest becomes the heavens well.

That's a paradox! Black is the color of hell, The hue of dungeons and the cloak of night; And yet you assert that your black-eyed beauty is heavenly.

BIRON
Devils soonest tempt, resembling spirits of light.
O, if in black my lady's brows be deck'd,
It mourns that painting and usurping hair
Should ravish doters with a false aspect;
And therefore is she born to make black fair.
Her favour turns the fashion of the days,
For native blood is counted painting now;
And therefore red, that would avoid dispraise,
Paints itself black, to imitate her brow.

The devil's temptation comes in the form of an angel of light. Of, if my lady's eyes are dressed in black, It's because they mourn that painted and false hair Would drive her suitors crazy for her with a false appearance; And so she is born to make black beautiful. Her face alters the fashion of the days, For a natural ruddy complexion is what women paint themselves to look like now; And so red, which wants to be praised, Paints itself black to imitate her.

DUMAIN
To look like her are chimney-sweepers black.

Chimney sweeps are also trying to look like her.

LONGAVILLE
And since her time are colliers counted bright.

And because of her, coal miners are called bright.

FERDINAND
And Ethiopes of their sweet complexion crack.

And Ethiopians boast of their sweet complexion.

DUMAIN
Dark needs no candles now, for dark is light.

No one needs candles anymore, since dark is now light.

BIRON
Your mistresses dare never come in rain,
For fear their colours should be wash'd away.

Your mistresses would never dare to be out in the rain, Afraid that all the painted colors on their face will get washed away.

FERDINAND
'Twere good, yours did; for, sir, to tell you plain,
I'll find a fairer face not wash'd to-day.

It would be good if yours did; I'll tell you plainly Even unwashed faces are prettier than hers.

BIRON
I'll prove her fair, or talk till doomsday here.

I'll prove to you that she is beautiful of talk here until doomsday.

FERDINAND
No devil will fright thee then so much as she.

No devil with scare you on doomsday as much as she will.

DUMAIN
I never knew man hold vile stuff so dear.

I've never know a man to hold something so vile with such affection.

LONGAVILLE
Look, here's thy love: my foot and her face see.

Look, here's your love: my foot is her face, see?

BIRON
O, if the streets were paved with thine eyes,
Her feet were much too dainty for such tread!

O, if the streets were paved with your eyes, Her feet would walk so daintily as to never hurt you!

DUMAIN
O, vile! then, as she goes, what upward lies
The street should see as she walk'd overhead.

O, gross! Well then as she walked, if my eyes are the street I'll be able to see up her skirt as she walks above me.

FERDINAND
But what of this? are we not all in love?

But what now? Aren't we all in love?

BIRON
Nothing so sure; and thereby all forsworn.

There's no doubt about it; we've all broken the oath.

FERDINAND
Then leave this chat; and, good Biron, now prove
Our loving lawful, and our faith not torn.

Then let's quit chatting; and, good Biron, now prove That our love is lawful, and that our faith is not torn.

DUMAIN
Ay, marry, there; some flattery for this evil.

Yes, that's right; we need some flattery for this evil.

LONGAVILLE

O, some authority how to proceed;
Some tricks, some quillets, how to cheat the
devil.

DUMAIN
Some salve for perjury.

BIRON
'Tis more than need.
Have at you, then, affection's men at arms.
Consider what you first did swear unto,
To fast, to study, and to see no woman;
Flat treason 'gainst the kingly state of youth.
Say, can you fast? your stomachs are too young;
And abstinence engenders maladies.
And where that you have vow'd to study, lords,
In that each of you have forsworn his book,
Can you still dream and pore and thereon look?
For when would you, my lord, or you, or you,
Have found the ground of study's excellence
Without the beauty of a woman's face?
From women's eyes this doctrine I derive;
They are the ground, the books, the academes
From whence doth spring the true Promethean
fire.
Why, universal plodding poisons up
The nimble spirits in the arteries,
As motion and long-during action tires
The sinewy vigour of the traveller.
Now, for not looking on a woman's face,
You have in that forsworn the use of eyes
And study too, the causer of your vow;
For where is any author in the world
Teaches such beauty as a woman's eye?
Learning is but an adjunct to ourself
And where we are our learning likewise is:
Then when ourselves we see in ladies' eyes,
Do we not likewise see our learning there?
O, we have made a vow to study, lords,
And in that vow we have forsworn our books.
For when would you, my liege, or you, or you,
In leaden contemplation have found out
Such fiery numbers as the prompting eyes
Of beauty's tutors have enrich'd you with?
Other slow arts entirely keep the brain;

O, some authority on how to proceed;
Some tricks, some verbal niceties and
distinctions, to cheat the devil.

Some ointment for this broken oath.

It's more than need.
I come at you with this, then, love's warriors.
Consider what you first swore to,
To fast, to study, and to see no woman;
That is flat treason against the kingly majesty of
youth. Tell me, can you fast? Your stomachs are
too young; And abstinence causes sicknesses.
And whereas you have vowed to study, lords,
Inasmuch as each of you have forsworn his
lady's face, Can you still dream and read and
look at it? Because when would you, my lord, or
you, or you, Have found the basis of study's
excellence Without the beauty of a woman's
face? From women's eyes I have obtained this
principle; They are the ground, the books, the
schools From which Prometheus' divine fire
springs.
Why, universal working and trudging poisons
The nimble spirits in the arteries,
Since motion and long-enduring action tires
The fibrous energy of the traveler.
Now, by not looking at a woman's face,
You have, in doing so, forsworn the use of the
eyes And study too, the whole reason for your
vow; For what author in the whole world
Teaches as much beauty as a woman's eye?
Learning is merely an addition to ourselves
And, likewise, our selves are an addition to our
learning: So then, when we see ourselves in our
ladies' eyes, Do we not also see our learning
there? O, we have made a vow to study, lords,
And in that vow we have forsworn our books.
For when would you, my liege, or you, or you,
In heavy contemplation have found out
Such fiery verses as the prompting eyes
Of beauty's tutors have enriched you with?
Other slow branches of knowledge dwell inside

And therefore, finding barren practisers,
Scarce show a harvest of their heavy toil:
But love, first learned in a lady's eyes,
Lives not alone immured in the brain;
But, with the motion of all elements,
Courses as swift as thought in every power,
And gives to every power a double power,
Above their functions and their offices.
It adds a precious seeing to the eye;
A lover's eyes will gaze an eagle blind;
A lover's ear will hear the lowest sound,
When the suspicious head of theft is stopp'd:
Love's feeling is more soft and sensible
Than are the tender horns of cockl'd snails;
Love's tongue proves dainty Bacchus gross in taste:
For valour, is not Love a Hercules,
Still climbing trees in the Hesperides?
Subtle as Sphinx; as sweet and musical
As bright Apollo's lute, strung with his hair:
And when Love speaks, the voice of all the gods
Makes heaven drowsy with the harmony.
Never durst poet touch a pen to write
Until his ink were temper'd with Love's sighs;
O, then his lines would ravish savage ears
And plant in tyrants mild humility.
From women's eyes this doctrine I derive:
They sparkle still the right Promethean fire;
They are the books, the arts, the academes,
That show, contain and nourish all the world:
Else none at all in ought proves excellent.
Then fools you were these women to forswear,
Or keeping what is sworn, you will prove fools.
For wisdom's sake, a word that all men love,
Or for love's sake, a word that loves all men,
Or for men's sake, the authors of these women,
Or women's sake, by whom we men are men,
Let us once lose our oaths to find ourselves,
Or else we lose ourselves to keep our oaths.
It is religion to be thus forsworn,
For charity itself fulfills the law,
And who can sever love from charity?

FERDINAND
Saint Cupid, then! and, soldiers, to the field!

the brain; And so, since we do not practice or use them, They barely show any harvest of their heavy toil: But love, first learned in a lady's eyes, Does not live alone confined in the brain; But, with the motion of all the elements, fire, earth, water, and air, Flows as swift as thought in every power, And gives every power a double power, Above and beyond their ordinary functions. It adds more precious seeing to the eye; A lover's eyes will out-gaze an eagle; A lover's ear will hear the lowest sound, Even when the most cautious thief hears nothing: A lover's senses are more soft and sensitive Than the tender little feelers on shelled snails; Love's tongue proves dainty Bacchus distasteful:

For bravery, isn't Love a Hercules, Still climbing trees in the Hesperides? Subtle as a Sphinx; as sweet and musical As bright Apollo's lute, strung with his own hair: And when Love speaks, the voice of all the gods Makes heaven sleepy with such beautiful harmony. Never has a poet dared touch his pen to write Until his ink is mixed with Love's sighs; O, then his lines would ravish savage ears And make tyrants humble.

From women's eyes I have obtained this principle: They still sparkle with the divine fire; They are the books, the arts, the schools, That show, contain, and nourish all the world: Otherwise nothing at all would be excellent. You were fools to forswear these women, Or if you keep to what you swore, you will prove to be fools. For the sake of wisdom, a word that all men love, Or for the sake of love, a word that inspires all men, Or for the sake of me, the authors of these women, Or for the sake of women, without whom we would not be men, Let's just this once, lose out oaths to find ourselves, Or else we lose ourselves to keep our oaths. It is religion to be forsworn like this, For the Bible says that charity itself fulfills the law, And who can separate love from charity?

For saint Cupid, then! And now, soldiers, to the field!

BIRON

Advance your standards, and upon them, lords;
Pell-mell, down with them! but be first advised,
In conflict that you get the sun of them.

Raise your flags and march, lords;
Attack them with reckless abandon! But make sure
That you get them with the sun in their eyes.

LONGAVILLE

Now to plain-dealing; lay these glozes by:
Shall we resolve to woo these girls of France?

Let's get down to business; lay these fallacies aside: Are we going to decide to woo these girls from France?

FERDINAND

And win them too: therefore let us devise
Some entertainment for them in their tents.

And win them too: so, let us plan
Some entertainment for them in their tents.

BIRON

First, from the park let us conduct them thither;
Then homeward every man attach the hand
Of his fair mistress: in the afternoon
We will with some strange pastime solace them,
Such as the shortness of the time can shape;
For revels, dances, masks and merry hours
Forerun fair Love, strewing her way with
flowers.

First, from the park we will take them there;
Then on the way home every man seize the hand
Of his fair lady: in the afternoon
We will comfort them with some strange
pastime, Whatever that short amount of time will
allow; For revels, dances, masks and cheerful
hours And beautiful Love will run ahead, paving
the way with flowers.

FERDINAND

Away, away! no time shall be omitted
That will betime, and may by us be fitted.

Come on, let's go! No time to waste
We need to take advantage of every minute.

BIRON

Allons! allons! Sow'd cockle reap'd no corn;
And justice always whirls in equal measure:
Light wenches may prove plagues to men
forsworn;
If so, our copper buys no better treasure.

Come on, come on! If you only plant weeds
you'll get no wheat; And justice always divvies
in equal portions: Frivolous girls may prove to
be plagues to men that are forsworn;
But beggars can't be choosers.

Exeunt

ACT V

SCENE I. The same.

Enter HOLOFERNES, SIR NATHANIEL, and DULL

HOLOFERNES
Satis quod sufficit.

Enough is as good as a feast.

SIR NATHANIEL
I praise God for you, sir: your reasons at dinner
have been sharp and sententious; pleasant
without
scurrility, witty without affection, audacious
without
impudency, learned without opinion, and
strange with-
out heresy. I did converse this quondam day
with
a companion of the king's, who is intituled,
nomi-
nated, or called, Don Adriano de Armado.

*I thank God for you, sir: your discourses at
dinner Have been sharp and moral; pleasant
without
Obscenity, witty without affection, fearless but
with
Respectfulness, educated without arrogance,
and novel
without heresy. I did converse the other day with
a companion of the king's who is titled, named,
Or called Don Adriano de Armado.*

HOLOFERNES
Novi hominem tanquam te: his humour is lofty,
his
discourse peremptory, his tongue filed, his eye
ambitious, his gait majestical, and his general
behavior vain, ridiculous, and thrasonical. He is
too picked, too spruce, too affected, too odd, as
it
were, too peregrinate, as I may call it.

*I know the man as well as I know you: his
attitude is lofty, his
Conversation imperious, his tongue polished,
his eye Ambitious, his walk majestic, and his
general Behavior vain, ridiculous, and boastful.
He is Too fastidious, too neat, too artificial, too
odd, as it
Were, too foreign, as I will call it.*

SIR NATHANIEL
A most singular and choice epithet.
Draws out his table-book

*A most remarkable and exquisite description.
Takes out his notebook*

HOLOFERNES
He draweth out the thread of his verbosity finer
than the staple of his argument. I abhor such
fanatical phantasimes, such insociable and
point-devise companions; such rackers of
orthography, as to speak dout, fine, when he
should
say doubt; det, when he should pronounce debt,-
-d,
e, b, t, not d, e, t: he clepeth a calf, cauf;

*He draws out the thread of his verbose words
finer Than the staple of his argument. I hate
such Fanatical people who enterain fantastic
notions, such unsociable and Extremely precise
fellows; such ruiners of Language, he says
'dout,' shortly, when he should
Say 'doubt'; 'det,' when he should pronounce
'debt,"*
E, b, t, not d, e, t: he calls a calf, 'cauf':

half, hauf; neighbour vocatur nebor; neigh
abbreviated ne. This is abhominable,--which he
would call abbominable: it insinuateth me of
insanie: anne intelligis, domine? to make frantic,
lunatic.

*Half, 'hauf'; neighbor is called 'nebor': neigh
Is abbreviated to 'ne.' This is abhominable, --
which he Would call abominable: To me is
sounds like Insanity. Do you understand me
master? To make frantic, lunatic.*

SIR NATHANIEL
Laus Deo, bene intelligo.

Praise be to God, I understand you well.

HOLOFERNES
Bon, bon, fort bon, Priscian! a little scratch'd,
'twill serve.

*Bon, bon, it should be 'bon'. Your latin is a little
faulty But it will serve.*

SIR NATHANIEL
Videsne quis venit?

Do you see who is coming?

HOLOFERNES
Video, et gaudeo.

I see, and I rejoice.

Enter DON ADRIANO DE ARMADO, MOTH, and COSTARD

DON ADRIANO DE ARMADO
Chirrah!

Chirrah!

To MOTH

HOLOFERNES
Quare chirrah, not sirrah?

Why chirrah, and not sirrah?

DON ADRIANO DE ARMADO
Men of peace, well encountered.

Men of peace, good to see you.

HOLOFERNES
Most military sir, salutation.

Most military, sir, greetings.

MOTH
[**Aside to COSTARD**] They have been at a
great feast
of languages, and stolen the scraps.

*[Aside to COSTARD] They just got back from a
huge feast
Of languages and have brought back the stolen
scraps.*

COSTARD
O, they have lived long on the alms-basket of
words.
I marvel thy master hath not eaten thee for a
word;
for thou art not so long by the head as

*O they have lives for a long time on the alms-
basket of words.
It's a wonder that your master has not eaten you
as a word;
Since you're not nearly as long as the word*

honorificabilitudinitatibus: thou art easier
swallowed than a flap-dragon.

honorificabilitudinitatibus: and you're easier
To swallow than a raisin.

MOTH
Peace! the peal begins.

Quiet! The clatter of tongues begins

DON ADRIANO DE ARMADO
[To HOLOFERNES] Monsieur, are you not
lettered?

[To HOLOFERNES] Sir, are you not educated?

MOTH
Yes, yes; he teaches boys the hornbook. What is
a,
b, spelt backward, with the horn on his head?

Yes, yes, he teaches boys the alphabet with the
book that's wrapped in a layer of horn.
What is a, b, spelled backward, with a horn on
its head?

HOLOFERNES
Ba, pueritia, with a horn added.

Ba, childish one, with a horn added.

MOTH
Ba, most silly sheep with a horn. You hear his
learning.

Ba what a silly sheep with a horn. You hear his
education.

HOLOFERNES
Quis, quis, thou consonant?

What, what, you consonant?

MOTH
The third of the five vowels, if you repeat them;
or
the fifth, if I.

The third of the five vowels, if you repeat them;
or
The fifth, if I do.

HOLOFERNES
I will repeat them,--a, e, i,--

I will repeat them, --a, e, i,--

MOTH
The sheep: the other two concludes it,--o, u.

You're the sheep: the other two concludes it, o,
u.

DON ADRIANO DE ARMADO
Now, by the salt wave of the Mediterraneum, a
sweet
touch, a quick venue of wit! snip, snap, quick
and
home! it rejoiceth my intellect: true wit!

Now, by the salty waves of the Mediterranean
sea, what a sweet
Touch, a quick show of wit! Snip, snap, quick
and
Then home! It is a joy to my intellect: true wit!

MOTH
Offered by a child to an old man; which is wit-

And it's told by a child to an old man; which is

old.   *mentally feeble.*

HOLOFERNES
What is the figure? what is the figure?   *What's the figure of speech there?*

MOTH
Horns.   *Horns.*

HOLOFERNES
Thou disputest like an infant: go, whip thy gig. *You reason like an infant: go, spin your top.*

MOTH
Lend me your horn to make one, and I will whip   *Lend me your horn to make one, and I will spin*
about   *around*
your infamy circum circa,--a gig of a cuckold's   *Your infamy with a ready hand, -- the top of a*
horn.   *cuckold's horn.*

COSTARD
An I had but one penny in the world, thou   *And if I had only one penny in the world, you*
shouldst   *should*
have it to buy gingerbread: hold, there is the   *Take it to buy gingerbread: wait, there is the*
very   *very*
remuneration I had of thy master, thou   *Remuneration I had of your master, your tiny*
halfpenny   *Purse of wit, you pigeon-egg of discretion. O,*
purse of wit, thou pigeon-egg of discretion. O,   *and*
an   *The heavens were so pleased that you were only*
the heavens were so pleased that thou wert but   *my*
my   *Bastard, what a joyful father you would make*
bastard, what a joyful father wouldst thou make   *me!*
me!   *Go to it; you have it ad dunghill, at the fingers'*
Go to; thou hast it ad dunghill, at the fingers' *Ends, as they say.*
ends, as they say.

HOLOFERNES
O, I smell false Latin; dunghill for unguem.   *O, I smell false Latin; he said dunghill instead*
                                                  of unguem.

DON ADRIANO DE ARMADO
Arts-man, preambulate, we will be singled from   *Scholar, walk with me, so we can be away from*
the   *these*
barbarous. Do you not educate youth at the   *Barbarians. Don't you educate the youth at the*
charge-house on the top of the mountain?   *School on the top of the mountain?*

HOLOFERNES
Or mons, the hill.   *It's more a hill.*

DON ADRIANO DE ARMADO

At your sweet pleasure, for the mountain.

If you prefer that over mountain.

HOLOFERNES
I do, sans question.

I do, without question.

DON ADRIANO DE ARMADO
Sir, it is the king's most sweet pleasure and affection to congratulate the princess at her pavilion in the posteriors of this day, which the rude multitude call the afternoon.

Sir, it is the king's great pleasure and
And affection to do the princess the honor of
paying her a visit At her pavilion in the rear end
of this day, which the Rude masses call the
afternoon.

HOLOFERNES
The posterior of the day, most generous sir, is liable, congruent and measurable for the afternoon:
the word is well culled, chose, sweet and apt, I do
assure you, sir, I do assure.

The rear end of the day, most generous sir, is
Apt, congruent, and fitted for the afternoon:
That word is well culled, well chosen, sweet and
apt, I do
Assure you, sir, I do assure.

DON ADRIANO DE ARMADO
Sir, the king is a noble gentleman, and my familiar,
I do assure ye, very good friend: for what is inward between us, let it pass. I do beseech thee, remember thy courtesy; I beseech thee, apparel thy
head: and among other important and most serious
designs, and of great import indeed, too, but let that pass: for I must tell thee, it will please his grace, by the world, sometime to lean upon my poor
shoulder, and with his royal finger, thus, dally with my excrement, with my mustachio; but, sweet
heart, let that pass. By the world, I recount no fable: some certain special honours it pleaseth his
greatness to impart to Armado, a soldier, a man of
travel, that hath seen the world; but let that pass. The very all of all is,--but, sweet heart, I do implore secrecy,--that the king would have me present the princess, sweet chuck, with some delightful ostentation, or show, or pageant, or

Sir, the king is a noble gentleman, and we are
very close,
I do assure you, a very good friend: for what is
Private between us, let it pass. I do ask you,
Remember that you have removed your hat; I
ask you, be sure to apparel
Your head: and among other important and very
serious
Clothes, and of great cost indeed, too, but let
That pass: for I must tell you, it will please his
Grace, sometimes to lean upon my poor
Shoulder, and with his royal finger, fix up
The outgrowth of my mustache; but sweet heart,
Let that pass. I promise, nothing I have said
Is untrue: some certain special honors it pleases
him
To bestow upon Armado, a soldier, a man of
Travel, that has seen the world; but let that
pass.
The very most of all of this, --but, sweet heart, I
do
Ask you for your secrecy, --that the king would
have me
Present the princess, sweet girl, with some
Delightful ostentation, or show, or pageant, or

antique, or firework. Now, understanding that the
curate and your sweet self are good at such
eruptions and sudden breaking out of mirth, as it
were, I have acquainted you withal, to the end to
crave your assistance.

Antique, or firework. Now, understanding that the
Clergyman and your sweet self are good at such
Eruptions and sudden breaking out of laughter,
as it Were, I have been getting acquainted with
you Because I crave your assistance.

HOLOFERNES
Sir, you shall present before her the Nine
Worthies.
Sir, as concerning some entertainment of time,
some
show in the posterior of this day, to be rendered
by
our assistants, at the king's command, and this
most
gallant, illustrate, and learned gentleman, before
the princess; I say none so fit as to present the
Nine Worthies.

Sir, you should present the Nine Worthies to her.
Sir, when it comes to some entertainment of
time, some
Show in the rear end of this day, to be rendered
by
Our assistants, at the king's command, and this
very
Gallant, good examples and educated
gentleman, for
The princess; I say that the best thing you could
present Is the Nine Worthies.

SIR NATHANIEL
Where will you find men worthy enough to
present them?

Where will you find men worthy enough to
represent them?

HOLOFERNES
Joshua, yourself; myself and this gallant
gentleman,
Judas Maccabaeus; this swain, because of his
great
limb or joint, shall pass Pompey the Great; the
page, Hercules,--

You will be Joshua, my and this gallant
gentleman will be
Judas Maccabaeus; ths country boy, because of
his great
Limb or joint will be Pompey the Great; the
Page, moth, will be Hercules,--

DON ADRIANO DE ARMADO
Pardon, sir; error: he is not quantity enough for
that Worthy's thumb: he is not so big as the end
of his club.

Pardon, sir, there's a mistake, he is not big
enough to be That Worthy's thumb: he is not
even as big as the end of his club.

HOLOFERNES
Shall I have audience? he shall present Hercules
in
minority: his enter and exit shall be strangling a
snake; and I will have an apology for that
purpose.

Will you hear me? He shall represent Hercules
as a
Baby: his entrance and exit shall be while he's
strangling a Snake; and I will have an
explanatory prologue for that purpose.

MOTH
An excellent device! so, if any of the audience

hiss, you may cry 'Well done, Hercules! now thou
crushest the snake!' that is the way to make an offence gracious, though few have the grace to do it.

DON ADRIANO DE ARMADO
For the rest of the Worthies?—

What about the rest of the Worthies?

HOLOFERNES
I will play three myself.

I will play three of them myself.

MOTH
Thrice-worthy gentleman!

A three times as worthy gentleman!

DON ADRIANO DE ARMADO
Shall I tell you a thing?

Can I tell you something?

HOLOFERNES
We attend.

We're listening.

DON ADRIANO DE ARMADO
We will have, if this fadge not, an antique. I beseech you, follow.

We will have, if this doesn't work, an antique. I Ask you, follow me.

HOLOFERNES
Via, goodman Dull! thou hast spoken no word all this while.

Hey, good man Dull! You haven't spoken a word this whole time.

DULL
Nor understood none neither, sir.

Nor did I understand one, sir.

HOLOFERNES
Allons! we will employ thee.

Come on! We will give you work to do!

DULL
I'll make one in a dance, or so; or I will play
On the tabour to the Worthies, and let them dance the hay.

*I'll be in a dance or something; or I will play
The drum to the Worthies and they can dance in the hay.*

HOLOFERNES
Most dull, honest Dull! To our sport, away!

How boring, honest Dull! To our task, let's go!

Exeunt
SCENE II. The same.

Enter the PRINCESS, KATHARINE, ROSALINE, and MARIA

PRINCESS
Sweet hearts, we shall be rich ere we depart,
If fairings come thus plentifully in:
A lady wall'd about with diamonds!
Look you what I have from the loving king.

My sweet hearts, we will be rich before we leave, If more of these complimentary gifts keep coming in: A lady surrounded by diamonds! Look at what I've gotten from the loving king.

ROSALINE
Madame, came nothing else along with that?

Madame, did nothing else come along with that?

PRINCESS
Nothing but this! yes, as much love in rhyme
As would be cramm'd up in a sheet of paper,
Writ o' both sides the leaf, margent and all,
That he was fain to seal on Cupid's name.

Nothing but this! yes, as much love written in rhyme As could possible be crammed onto a sheet of paper, Written on both sides, in the margins and everything, That he had to place the seal on top of Cupid's name.

ROSALINE
That was the way to make his godhead wax,
For he hath been five thousand years a boy.

That was the way to make his deity increase, For he has been a boy for five thousand years.

KATHARINE
Ay, and a shrewd unhappy gallows too.

Yes, and a wicked mischievous scoundrel who deserves to be hanged, too.

ROSALINE
You'll ne'er be friends with him; a' kill'd your
sister.

You'll never be friends with him; he killed your sister.

KATHARINE
He made her melancholy, sad, and heavy;
And so she died: had she been light, like you,
Of such a merry, nimble, stirring spirit,
She might ha' been a grandam ere she died:
And so may you; for a light heart lives long.

He made her melancholy, sad, and heavy; And so she died: if she was light, like you, With a cheerful, nimble, and energetic spirit, She might have been a grandmother before she died: And so might you; since a light heart lives long.

ROSALINE
What's your dark meaning, mouse, of this light
word?

What's the dark meaning, little mouse, behind the word 'light'?

KATHARINE
A light condition in a beauty dark.

A lustful temperament and a dark beauty.

ROSALINE

We need more light to find your meaning out.

You need to enlighten us to your meaning.

KATHARINE
You'll mar the light by taking it in snuff;
Therefore I'll darkly end the argument.

You'll ruin the light by taking offence;
And so I will darkly end the argument.

ROSALINE
Look what you do, you do it still i' the dark.

Whatever you do, you do it still in the dark.

KATHARINE
So do not you, for you are a light wench.

And you don't, since you're an easy wench.

ROSALINE
Indeed I weigh not you, and therefore light.

I don't weigh as much as you do, so yes, I'm light.

KATHARINE
You weigh me not? O, that's you care not for me.

You don't take me seriously? You don't care about me.

ROSALINE
Great reason; for 'past cure is still past care.'

Well since you are past curing, you are past caring for.

PRINCESS
Well bandied both; a set of wit well play'd.
But Rosaline, you have a favour too:
Who sent it? and what is it?

Well said, both of you; a set of wit well played.
But Rosaline, you have a love token as well:
Who sent it? And what is it?

ROSALINE
I would you knew:
An if my face were but as fair as yours,
My favour were as great; be witness this.
Nay, I have verses too, I thank Biron:
The numbers true; and, were the numbering too,
I were the fairest goddess on the ground:
I am compared to twenty thousand fairs.
O, he hath drawn my picture in his letter!

I wish you knew:
And if only my face was as fair as yours,
My gift would be as great; be witness to this.
And, I have verses too, I thank Biron:
The meter is true; and, if the reckoning were
too, I would be the fairest goddess on the
ground: I am compared to twenty thousand
beautiful women. With this letter he has drawn
an image of me!

PRINCESS
Any thing like?

Is it any likeness?

ROSALINE
Much in the letters; nothing in the praise.

Much in the actual lettering; nothing alike in the praise.

PRINCESS
Beauteous as ink; a good conclusion.

As beautiful as black ink; a good conclusion.

KATHARINE
Fair as a text B in a copy-book.

Beautiful like a black printed letter B in a book.

ROSALINE
'Ware pencils, ho! let me not die your debtor,
My red dominical, my golden letter:
O, that your face were not so full of O's!

Have at you in this skirmish of satirical
portraits, don't let me die in your debt,
My red-faced and golden lettered one:
O, if only your face were not so full of O's!

KATHARINE
A pox of that jest! and I beshrew all shrows.

That's from smallpox! And I curse all shrews.

PRINCESS
But, Katharine, what was sent to you from fair
Dumain?

But, Katharine, what was sent to you from good
Dumain?

KATHARINE
Madam, this glove.

Madam, this glove.

PRINCESS
Did he not send you twain?

Didn't he send over its twin?

KATHARINE
Yes, madam, and moreover
Some thousand verses of a faithful lover,
A huge translation of hypocrisy,
Vilely compiled, profound simplicity.

Yes, madam, and moreover
About a thousand verses of a faithful lover,
A huge translation of hypocrisy,
Horribly compiled, profound stupidity.

MARIA
This and these pearls to me sent Longaville:
The letter is too long by half a mile.

This and these pearls were sent to me by
Longaville: The letter is too long by half a mile.

PRINCESS
I think no less. Dost thou not wish in heart
The chain were longer and the letter short?

I think the same thing. Don't you wish in your
heart That the string of pearls was longer and
the letter was shorter?

MARIA
Ay, or I would these hands might never part.

Yes, or I wouldn't want to marry..

PRINCESS
We are wise girls to mock our lovers so.

We are such smart girls to make fun of our
lovers like this.

ROSALINE
They are worse fools to purchase mocking so.
That same Biron I'll torture ere I go:
O that I knew he were but in by the week!
How I would make him fawn and beg and seek

They are worse fools to get themselves mocked
like this. That Biron man, I'll torture before I
go: O If I knew that he was trapped
permanently! I would make him fawn over me

And wait the season and observe the times
And spend his prodigal wits in bootless rhymes
And shape his service wholly to my hests
And make him proud to make me proud that jests!
So perttaunt-like would I o'ersway his state
That he should be my fool and I his fate.

PRINCESS
None are so surely caught, when they are catch'd,
As wit turn'd fool: folly, in wisdom hatch'd,
Hath wisdom's warrant and the help of school
And wit's own grace to grace a learned fool.

ROSALINE
The blood of youth burns not with such excess
As gravity's revolt to wantonness.

MARIA
Folly in fools bears not so strong a note
As foolery in the wise, when wit doth dote;
Since all the power thereof it doth apply
To prove, by wit, worth in simplicity.

PRINCESS
Here comes Boyet, and mirth is in his face.

Enter BOYET

BOYET
O, I am stabb'd with laughter! Where's her grace?

PRINCESS
Thy news Boyet?

BOYET
Prepare, madam, prepare!
Arm, wenches, arm! encounters mounted are
Against your peace: Love doth approach disguised,
Armed in arguments; you'll be surprised:
Muster your wits; stand in your own defence;
Or hide your heads like cowards, and fly hence.

and beg and seek And wait through the seasons and watch time go by And spend his extravagant wits in fruitless rhymes And make him my slave And make him take satisfaction in glorifying me, the one who makes fun of him
And like holding a winning hand at cards, I would oversway his state
So that he would be my fool and I his fate.

No one is as surely caught, when then are caught,
As wit that is turned foolish: recklessness that comes from wisdom, Has wisdom's permission and the help of schooling And the gift of wit to grace an educated fool.

The blood of youth does not burn with such excess
As a wise man's rebellion to being unrestrained.

Recklessness in fools is not as strong
As foolery in the wise, when wit grows fond;
Since all of its power is then applied
To prove, by wit, their worth in foolishness.

Here comes Boyet, and cheerfulness in his face.

O I am stabbed with laughter! Where is her grace?

What is your news Boyet?

Prepare yourself, madam, prepare yourself!
Arm yourselves, girls! The mounted confronters Are against your peace: Love approaches, disguised,
Armed with arguments; you will be overcome by surprise attack: Rally your wits; stand and defend yourselves; Or hide your heads like

PRINCESS

Saint Denis to Saint Cupid! What are they
That charge their breath against us? say, scout,
say.

coward, and run from here.

*Saint Denis to Saint Cupid! What are they
That are charging this way to meet us? Tell us,
scout.*

BOYET

Under the cool shade of a sycamore
I thought to close mine eyes some half an hour;
When, lo! to interrupt my purposed rest,
Toward that shade I might behold addrest
The king and his companions: warily
I stole into a neighbour thicket by,
And overheard what you shall overhear,
That, by and by, disguised they will be here.
Their herald is a pretty knavish page,
That well by heart hath conn'd his embassage:
Action and accent did they teach him there;
'Thus must thou speak,' and 'thus thy body bear:'
And ever and anon they made a doubt
Presence majestical would put him out,
'For,' quoth the king, 'an angel shalt thou see;
Yet fear not thou, but speak audaciously.'
The boy replied, 'An angel is not evil;
I should have fear'd her had she been a devil.'
With that, all laugh'd and clapp'd him on the
shoulder,
Making the bold wag by their praises bolder:
One rubb'd his elbow thus, and fleer'd and swore
A better speech was never spoke before;
Another, with his finger and his thumb,
Cried, 'Via! we will do't, come what will come;'
The third he caper'd, and cried, 'All goes well;'
The fourth turn'd on the toe, and down he fell.
With that, they all did tumble on the ground,
With such a zealous laughter, so profound,
That in this spleen ridiculous appears,
To cheque their folly, passion's solemn tears.

*Under the cool shade of a sycamore tree
I was planning to take a nap for about half an
hour; When, suddenly! Interrupting my planned
rest, Toward that shade I could see approaching
The king and his companions: warily
I hid in a nearby thicket,
And overheard what I will tell you now,
Which is that pretty soon they will be here in
disguise. Their announcer is a pretty crafty
page, That has learned by heart his message:
They taught him gestures and accent
'Say it like this' and 'make your body do this:'
And every now and again they expressed a fear
That your majestic presence would discomfort
him, 'Since,' said the king, 'you will see an
angel; yet don't be afraid, but speak boldly.'
The boy replied, 'An angel is not evil;
I would have be afraid of her if she was a devil.'
With that, they all laughed and clapped him on
the shoulder,
Making the brave little joker bolder with their
praises: One rubbed his elbow then, and
grinned and swore That a better speech has
never been spoken before; Another, snapping
his fingers, Cried, 'Let's go! We will do it, come
what may;' The third he leapt playfully and
cried, 'All goes well;' The fourth turned on the
toe, and fell down. With that, they all tumbled to
the ground, With such energetic laughter, so
profound, That in this excess of laughter
appears, In order to keep their silliness in check,
passion's solemn tears in their eyes.*

PRINCESS

But what, but what, come they to visit us?

*And what? And what, are they coming to visit
us?*

BOYET

They do, they do: and are apparell'd thus.
Like Muscovites or Russians, as I guess.
Their purpose is to parle, to court and dance;

*They are, they are: and they are dressed
Like Muscovites or Russians, is my guess.
Their purpose is to talk, to court, and dance;*

And every one his love-feat will advance
Unto his several mistress, which they'll know
By favours several which they did bestow.

PRINCESS
And will they so? the gallants shall be task'd;
For, ladies, we shall every one be mask'd;
And not a man of them shall have the grace,
Despite of suit, to see a lady's face.
Hold, Rosaline, this favour thou shalt wear,
And then the king will court thee for his dear;
Hold, take thou this, my sweet, and give me thine,
So shall Biron take me for Rosaline.
And change your favours too; so shall your loves
Woo contrary, deceived by these removes.

ROSALINE
Come on, then; wear the favours most in sight.

KATHARINE
But in this changing what is your intent?

PRINCESS
The effect of my intent is to cross theirs:
They do it but in mocking merriment;
And mock for mock is only my intent.
Their several counsels they unbosom shall
To loves mistook, and so be mock'd withal
Upon the next occasion that we meet,
With visages displayed, to talk and greet.

ROSALINE
But shall we dance, if they desire to't?

PRINCESS
No, to the death, we will not move a foot;
Nor to their penn'd speech render we no grace,
But while 'tis spoke each turn away her face.

BOYET
Why, that contempt will kill the speaker's heart,
And quite divorce his memory from his part.

And every one of them will perform a feat of love For his severe mistress, which they will know By all the tokens that they have bestowed.

Oh, will they now? The gallant men shall be put to the task; For ladies, every one of us will be masked; And not a man of them shall have the pleasure, Despite our clothes, to see a lady's face. Rosaline, you will wear this token, And then the king will court you as his dear; Here, you take this, my sweet, and give me yours, So Biron will think that I am Rosaline. And you two exchange your gifts too; so your loves Will woo the wrong one, deceived by the switch.

Come on, then; make sure your wear the gifts where they are in plain sight.

But what's your intent in this changing?

The effect of my intent is to test theirs: They only do it for fun, to mock us; And my intent is only to mock them back. And their private intentions and they confide To their mistaken loves, will be mocked moreover On the next time that we meet, With our faces exposed, to talk and greet.

But should we dance, if they as us to?

No, on pain of death, we won't budge one foot; And when they read their speeches we will give them no politeness, But while it is spoken each turn away her face.

Why something so cruel will kill the speaker's heart, And very much separate his memory from his chosen lady.

PRINCESS

Therefore I do it; and I make no doubt
The rest will ne'er come in, if he be out
There's no such sport as sport by sport
o'erthrown,
To make theirs ours and ours none but our own:
So shall we stay, mocking intended game,
And they, well mock'd, depart away with shame.

*That's why I will do it; and I don't doubt
That the rest will never come in, if he is
comfused There's no game more fun than
someone's game being overthrown by yours,
To make their fun ours, and ours only fun for
ourselves: That's what we'll so, making fun of
their little game, And they, well mocked, will
leave in shame.*

Trumpets sound within

BOYET

The trumpet sounds: be mask'd; the maskers
come.
The Ladies mask

*The trumpet sounds: get your masks on; the
maskers come.
The Ladies put their masks on*

**Enter Blackamoors with music; MOTH; FERDINAND, BIRON, LONGAVILLE, and
DUMAIN, in Russian habits, and masked**

MOTH

All hail, the richest beauties on the earth!—

All hail, the richest beauties on the earth!---

BOYET

Beauties no richer than rich taffeta.

*Beauties that are no richer than a mask made of
taffeta cloth.*

MOTH

A holy parcel of the fairest dames.

A holy company of the lovliest dames.

The Ladies turn their backs to him

That ever turn'd their--backs--to mortal views!

That ever turned their—backs—to mortal views!

BIRON

[Aside to MOTH] Their eyes, villain, their eyes!

*[Aside to MOTH] Their eyes, you idiot, their
eyes!*

MOTH

That ever turn'd their eyes to mortal views!--
Out—

*That ever turned their eyes to mortal views! –
Out---*

BOYET

True; out indeed.

True; outright confused.

MOTH

Out of your favours, heavenly spirits, vouchsafe
Not to behold—

*Out of your tokens, heavenly angels, condescend
to grant Not to behold---*

BIRON
[Aside to MOTH] Once to behold, rogue.

[Aside to MOHT] Once to behold, dummy.

MOTH
Once to behold with your sun-beamed eyes,
--with your sun-beamed eyes—

Once to behold with your sun-beamed eyes,
--with your sun-beamed eyes--

BOYET
They will not answer to that epithet;
You were best call it 'daughter-beamed eyes.'

They will not answer to that description;
You had better call it 'Daighter-beamed eyes.'

MOTH
They do not mark me, and that brings me out.

They're not listening to me, and that puts me
out.

BIRON
Is this your perfectness? be gone, you rogue!

Is this your so-called perfection? Get out of
here, you scoundrel!

Exit MOTH

ROSALINE
What would these strangers? know their minds,
Boyet:
If they do speak our language, 'tis our will:
That some plain man recount their purposes
Know what they would.

What do these strangers want? Figure out why
they're here, Boyet:
If they can speak our language, it is our wish
That some plain-speaking man tell us their
purposes And tell us what they want.

BOYET
What would you with the princess?

What do you want with the princess?

BIRON
Nothing but peace and gentle visitation.

Nothing but peace and gentle visitation.

ROSALINE
What would they, say they?

What did they say they want?

BOYET
Nothing but peace and gentle visitation.

Nothing but peace and gentle visitation.

ROSALINE
Why, that they have; and bid them so be gone.

Well, the have that; now tell them to leave.

BOYET
She says, you have it, and you may be gone.

She says you have it, and you can leave.

FERDINAND

104

Say to her, we have measured many miles
To tread a measure with her on this grass.

BOYET
They say, that they have measured many a mile
To tread a measure with you on this grass.

ROSALINE
It is not so. Ask them how many inches
Is in one mile: if they have measured many,
The measure then of one is easily told.

BOYET
If to come hither you have measured miles,
And many miles, the princess bids you tell
How many inches doth fill up one mile.

BIRON
Tell her, we measure them by weary steps.

BOYET
She hears herself.

ROSALINE
How many weary steps,
Of many weary miles you have o'ergone,
Are number'd in the travel of one mile?

BIRON
We number nothing that we spend for you:
Our duty is so rich, so infinite,
That we may do it still without accompt.
Vouchsafe to show the sunshine of your face,
That we, like savages, may worship it.

ROSALINE
My face is but a moon, and clouded too.

FERDINAND
Blessed are clouds, to do as such clouds do!
Vouchsafe, bright moon, and these thy stars, to shine,
Those clouds removed, upon our watery eyne.

ROSALINE
O vain petitioner! beg a greater matter;

Say to her that we have traveled many miles
To dance with her on this grass.

They say that they have come a long ways
To dance with you on this grass.

That's not true. Ask them how many inches
Are in one mile: if they have walked many miles,
Then they can easily say how many.

If to get here you have some many miles,
The princess asks you to tell her
How many inches are in a mile.

Tell her that we measure them by weary steps.

She hears you herself.

How many weary steps,
Of the many weary miles you have traveled,
Are numbered in the travel of one mile?

We don't count anything that we spend for you:
Our task is so rich, so infinite,
That we do it without calculating.
Condescend to grant us the pleasure, show the
sunshine of your face, So that we, like savages,
may worship it.

My face is only a moon, and masked too.

What lucky clouds to be so close as to mask your
face! Grant us the privilege, bright moon, and
these, your stars, to shine,
With the clouds removed, upon our watery eyes.

O, what a vain request! Beg for a greater

Thou now request'st but moonshine in the water.

purpose; What you're asking for now is nothing at all.

FERDINAND
Then, in our measure do but vouchsafe one change.
Thou bid'st me beg: this begging is not strange.

Well then, if you would, grant us one dance.
You asked me to beg: this request is not strange.

ROSALINE
Play, music, then! Nay, you must do it soon.

Play music, then! And you must do it soon,

Music plays

Not yet! no dance! Thus change I like the moon.

Not yet! No dance! So I change like the moon.

FERDINAND
Will you not dance? How come you thus estranged?

You won't dance? How did you become so estranged?

ROSALINE
You took the moon at full, but now she's changed.

You took a full moon, but now she's changed.

FERDINAND
Yet still she is the moon, and I the man.
The music plays; vouchsafe some motion to it.

But she is still the moon, and I the man in the moon. The music plays; grant some motion to it.

ROSALINE
Our ears vouchsafe it.

Our ears grant it.

FERDINAND
But your legs should do it.

But your legs should do it.

ROSALINE
Since you are strangers and come here by chance,
We'll not be nice: take hands. We will not dance.

Since you are strangers and have come here by chance,
We will not be coy: take my hand. We will not dance.

FERDINAND
Why take we hands, then?

Why should I take your hand then?

ROSALINE
Only to part friends:
Curtsy, sweet hearts; and so the measure ends.

So that we may part friends:
Curtsy, ladies; and so the dance ends.

FERDINAND
More measure of this measure; be not nice.

We wish more of this dance; don't be coy.

ROSALINE
We can afford no more at such a price.

We can afford no more at such a price.

FERDINAND
Prize you yourselves: what buys your company?

Name your price: what buys your company?

ROSALINE
Your absence only.

Only your absence.

FERDINAND
That can never be.

That can't be.

ROSALINE
Then cannot we be bought: and so, adieu;
Twice to your visor, and half once to you.

Then we cannot be bought: and so, goodbye;
Twice to your mask and half to you.

FERDINAND
If you deny to dance, let's hold more chat.

If you won't dance, let's at least talk.

ROSALINE
In private, then.

In private then.

FERDINAND
I am best pleased with that.

That's what I would prefer.

They converse apart

BIRON
White-handed mistress, one sweet word with
thee.

White-handed mistress, I ask for one sweet word
with you.

PRINCESS
Honey, and milk, and sugar; there is three.

Honey, milk, sugar; there that's three words.

BIRON
Nay then, two treys, and if you grow so nice,
Metheglin, wort, and malmsey: well run, dice!
There's half-a-dozen sweets.

No then, two threes, and if you are going to be
so subtle, Tea, beer, wine: that was a good roll
of the dice! That makes half a dozen sweet
things we have listed.

PRINCESS
Seventh sweet, adieu:
Since you can cog, I'll play no more with you.

The seventh sweet is goodbye:
Since you can cheat, I'll play no more with you.

BIRON
One word in secret.

One word in secret.

PRINCESS
Let it not be sweet.

As long as it's not sweet.

BIRON
Thou grievest my gall.

You sadden my boldness.

PRINCESS
Gall! bitter.

Gall! Gall is bitter.

BIRON
Therefore meet.

Therefore fitting.

They converse apart

DUMAIN
Will you vouchsafe with me to change a word?

Will you grant me the privilege of changing words with me?

MARIA
Name it.

Name it.

DUMAIN
Fair lady,--

Fair lady,--

MARIA
Say you so? Fair lord,--
Take that for your fair lady.

Is that the word? Fair lord,--
That's what I'll change Fair lady to.

DUMAIN
Please it you,
As much in private, and I'll bid adieu.

If it please you,
You can say that much in private and I'll say goodbye afterwards.

They converse apart

KATHARINE
What, was your vizard made without a tongue?

What, was your mask made without a tongue?

LONGAVILLE
I know the reason, lady, why you ask.

I know why you say that, my lady.

KATHARINE
O for your reason! quickly, sir; I long.

O, let me hear your reason! quickly sir, I long to hear it.

LONGAVILLE
You have a double tongue within your mask,
And would afford my speechless vizard half.

You have a double tongue within your mask,
And talk enough for the both of us.

KATHARINE
Veal, quoth the Dutchman. Is not 'veal' a calf?

'Veal' said the Dutchman. Isn't veal a calf?

LONGAVILLE
A calf, fair lady!

A calf, fair lady!

KATHARINE
No, a fair lord calf.

No, a fair lord calf.

LONGAVILLE
Let's part the word.

Let's split that word between us.

KATHARINE
No, I'll not be your half
Take all, and wean it; it may prove an ox.

No I won't be your other half
Take the whole calf and it could turn out to
actually be an ox.

LONGAVILLE
Look, how you butt yourself in these sharp
mocks!
Will you give horns, chaste lady? do not so.

Look how you injure yourself with these sharp
insults!
Will you act so agressively, abstinent lady?
Please don't.

KATHARINE
Then die a calf, before your horns do grow.

Then die a calf, before you've grown up.

LONGAVILLE
One word in private with you, ere I die.

One word in private with you, before I die.

KATHARINE
Bleat softly then; the butcher hears you cry.

Bleat softly then little calf; or else the butcher
will find you.

They converse apart

BOYET
The tongues of mocking wenches are as keen
As is the razor's edge invisible,
Cutting a smaller hair than may be seen,
Above the sense of sense; so sensible
Seemeth their conference; their conceits have
wings
Fleeter than arrows, bullets, wind, thought,
swifter things.

The tongues of joking women are as sharply
insulting As the razor's edge is invisible,
and can cut a hair so small it can't be seen,
beyond the ability of the senses; so quick-witted
seems their conversation; their desires have
wings
faster than arrows, bullets, wind, thought and
things swifter than that even.

ROSALINE
Not one word more, my maids; break off, break off.

Don't speak another word, my maids; break off this conversation, break it off.

BIRON
By heaven, all dry-beaten with pure scoff!

By heaven, we're all beaten soundly without blood drawn by your scoffing.

FERDINAND
Farewell, mad wenches; you have simple wits.

Goodbye, crazy ladies; you are dim-witted.

PRINCESS
Twenty adieus, my frozen Muscovits.

Twenty goodbyes, my cold Muscovites.

Exeunt FERDINAND, Lords, and Blackamoors

Are these the breed of wits so wonder'd at?

Are these guys so witty as everyone says?

BOYET
Tapers they are, with your sweet breaths puff'd out.

Diminished they are, when you speak.

ROSALINE
Well-liking wits they have; gross, gross; fat, fat.

Their wits are plump and in good-condition; gross, gross; fat, fat.

PRINCESS
O poverty in wit, kingly-poor flout!
Will they not, think you, hang themselves tonight?
Or ever, but in vizards, show their faces?
This pert Biron was out of countenance quite.

O poor in wit, poor mockery of the king! Don't you think they will hang themselves tonight? Or ever show their faces without masks on? This impertinent Biron seemed quite upset.

ROSALINE
O, they were all in lamentable cases!
The king was weeping-ripe for a good word.

O, they were all in pathetic states! The king was ready to weep to earn a kind word.

PRINCESS
Biron did swear himself out of all suit.

Biron did swear himself excessively and to no avail.

MARIA
Dumain was at my service, and his sword:
No point, quoth I; my servant straight was mute.

Dumain claimed to be at my service, and his sword: I said was dull and blunted; that shut him up.

KATHARINE
Lord Longaville said, I came o'er his heart;
And trow you what he called me?

Lord Longaville said, I came over his heart; And can you guess what he called me?

110

PRINCESS
Qualm, perhaps.

A heartsickness, perhaps.

KATHARINE
Yes, in good faith.

Yes, you guessed it.

PRINCESS
Go, sickness as thou art!

Go, sickness that you are!

ROSALINE
Well, better wits have worn plain statute-caps.
But will you hear? the king is my love sworn.

*Well, one could find better wits among
apprentices. But will you listen to me? The king
swore his love to me.*

PRINCESS
And quick Biron hath plighted faith to me.

*And fast-talking Biron has claimed to be faithful
to me.*

KATHARINE
And Longaville was for my service born.

And Longaville was born to serve me.

MARIA
Dumain is mine, as sure as bark on tree.

Dumain is mine, as bark is to a tree.

BOYET
Madam, and pretty mistresses, give ear:
Immediately they will again be here
In their own shapes; for it can never be
They will digest this harsh indignity.

*Madam, and pretty mistresses, please listen:
They will soon be here again
Without masks; for they will never be
able to deal with this humiliation.*

PRINCESS
Will they return?

Will they return?

BOYET
They will, they will, God knows,
And leap for joy, though they are lame with
blows:
Therefore change favours; and, when they
repair,
Blow like sweet roses in this summer air.

*They will, they will, God knows,
and they will leap for joy, though they have been
beaten down:
Therefore switch the charms that they will
identify you by, and when they come back,
You will bloom like sweet roses in the summer
air.*

PRINCESS
How blow? how blow? speak to be understood.

*What do you mean bloom? bloom? Speak so I
can understand you.*

BOYET
Fair ladies mask'd are roses in their bud;
Dismask'd, their damask sweet commixture
shown,

*Fair ladies, roses are concealed in their bud;
Unmasked their mingling red and white mixture
is shown,*

Are angels vailing clouds, or roses blown.

As are angels in the clouds, or roses blooming.

PRINCESS
Avaunt, perplexity! What shall we do,
If they return in their own shapes to woo?

Away, riddler! Tell us what to do,
If they return without their masks to woo us?

ROSALINE
Good madam, if by me you'll be advised,
Let's, mock them still, as well known as
disguised:
Let us complain to them what fools were here,
Disguised like Muscovites, in shapeless gear;
And wonder what they were and to what end
Their shallow shows and prologue vilely penn'd
And their rough carriage so ridiculous,
Should be presented at our tent to us.

Good madam, if you'll let me advise you,
Let's continue to mock them, as we know they
are disguised:
Let us complain to them about the fools that
were here, Disguised like Muscovites, in
unshapely apparel; And we will wonder aloud
who they were and what they wanted Their
shallowness shows and their actions vilely
motivated And the way they carry themselves so
ridiculous, Should be shown to us at our tent.

BOYET
Ladies, withdraw: the gallants are at hand.

Ladies, go to your tents: the men are coming
back.

PRINCESS
Whip to our tents, as roes run o'er land.

Quickly let's go to our tents, as swiftly as deer
run over land.

Exeunt PRINCESS, ROSALINE, KATHARINE, and MARIA

Re-enter FERDINAND, BIRON, LONGAVILLE, and DUMAIN, in their proper habits

FERDINAND
Fair sir, God save you! Where's the princess?

Fair sir, God save you! Where's the princess?

BOYET
Gone to her tent. Please it your majesty
Command me any service to her thither?

She's gone to her tent. Would it please your
majesty To command me to go ask anything of
her there?

FERDINAND
That she vouchsafe me audience for one word.

That she would allow me to speak to her.

BOYET
I will; and so will she, I know, my lord.

I will; and I know she will too, my lord.

Exit

BIRON
This fellow pecks up wit as pigeons pease,

This guy gathers wit as pigeons eat peas,

And utters it again when God doth please:
He is wit's pedler, and retails his wares
At wakes and wassails, meetings, markets, fairs;
And we that sell by gross, the Lord doth know,
Have not the grace to grace it with such show.
This gallant pins the wenches on his sleeve;
Had he been Adam, he had tempted Eve;
A' can carve too, and lisp: why, this is he
That kiss'd his hand away in courtesy;
This is the ape of form, monsieur the nice,
That, when he plays at tables, chides the dice
In honourable terms: nay, he can sing
A mean most meanly; and in ushering
Mend him who can: the ladies call him sweet;
The stairs, as he treads on them, kiss his feet:
This is the flower that smiles on every one,
To show his teeth as white as whale's bone;
And consciences, that will not die in debt,
Pay him the due of honey-tongued Boyet.

And is able to speak wittily whenever God pleases: He is a salesman of wit, and sells his goods At funerals and parties, meetings, markets, and fairs; And we that buy it at cost, the Lord knows, Don't have the grace to do it justice He flaunts his success with women like they were charms on a bracelet If he had been Adam, he would have tempted Eve with the apple; And he can woo with his affability too: why, this is he that gives his hand as a courtesy This is the ape of manners, master of the demanding, That, when he gambles, he lectures the dice About their honor: No, he can sing with a fairly decent voice; and in being a gentleman allows anyone who can improve him to do so: the ladies say he's sweet; The stairs kiss his feet as he walks on them: This is the flower that smiles at every one, To show how his teeth are as white as a whale's bone; And anyone who doesn't want to be in debt to anyone, Pay what is owed to sweet-talking Boyet

FERDINAND
A blister on his sweet tongue, with my heart,
That put Armado's page out of his part!

I hope he gets a blister on his sweet tongue, Since he put Armado's page out of his part!

BIRON
See where it comes! Behavior, what wert thou
Till this madman show'd thee? and what art thou
now?

Look where Boyet comes! What were your manners like before you started acting like a madman? And how do you behave now?

Re-enter the PRINCESS, ushered by BOYET, ROSALINE, MARIA, and KATHARINE

FERDINAND
All hail, sweet madam, and fair time of day!

All hail, sweet madam, and what a great day it is!

PRINCESS
'Fair' in 'all hail' is foul, as I conceive.

I believe you mean 'hail' as in a hail storm.

FERDINAND
Construe my speeches better, if you may.

Please understand I mean to speak well for you.

PRINCESS
Then wish me better; I will give you leave.

Then greet me better; or I will leave.

FERDINAND
We came to visit you, and purpose now

We came to see you, with the purpose of

To lead you to our court; vouchsafe it then.

bringing you to our court; Please grant me that.

PRINCESS
This field shall hold me; and so hold your vow:
Nor God, nor I, delights in perjured men.

We can speak here just as well; and so keep your promise: Neither God, nor myself, take pleasure in liars.

FERDINAND
Rebuke me not for that which you provoke:
The virtue of your eye must break my oath.

Don't get on to me for that which you instigated: The power of your eye makes me break my promise.

PRINCESS
You nickname virtue; vice you should have spoke;
For virtue's office never breaks men's troth.
Now by my maiden honour, yet as pure
As the unsullied lily, I protest,
A world of torments though I should endure,
I would not yield to be your house's guest;
So much I hate a breaking cause to be
Of heavenly oaths, vow'd with integrity.

*You use the word virtue; but you should have said vice;
For virtue never causes a man to break his promise. Now as I am a lady, and a pure virgin like a lily, I refuse,
Even if I had were tortured,
I wouldn't go to your house;
Because I hate to be the reason for breaking heavenly promises, that were sworn with integrity.*

FERDINAND
O, you have lived in desolation here,
Unseen, unvisited, much to our shame.

*O, you don't get out much,
You don't see anyone, no one visits you, which is a shame.*

PRINCESS
Not so, my lord; it is not so, I swear;
We have had pastimes here and pleasant game:
A mess of Russians left us but of late.

That's not true, my lord; It's not the case, I swear; We have entertained here and played games: Four Russians have only just left.

FERDINAND
How, madam! Russians!

What! Russians!

PRINCESS
Ay, in truth, my lord;
Trim gallants, full of courtship and of state.

*Yes, it's true, my lord;
Fit, gallant men of stature who wanted to court me.*

ROSALINE
Madam, speak true. It is not so, my lord:
My lady, to the manner of the days,
In courtesy gives undeserving praise.
We four indeed confronted were with four
In Russian habit: here they stay'd an hour,
And talk'd apace; and in that hour, my lord,
They did not bless us with one happy word.

*Madam, tell the truth. That's not the case, my lord: My lady, like the days pass,
gives praise where it is undeserved just to be nice. The four of us did meet four men
In Russian clothes: they stayed here an hour,
And talked a bit; and in an hour, my lord,
They did not say one nice thing to us.*

I dare not call them fools; but this I think,
When they are thirsty, fools would fain have drink.

I wouldn't say they were fools; but I do think,
When fools are thirsty they would like to have a drink.

BIRON
This jest is dry to me. Fair gentle sweet,
Your wit makes wise things foolish: when we greet,
With eyes best seeing, heaven's fiery eye,
By light we lose light: your capacity
Is of that nature that to your huge store
Wise things seem foolish and rich things but poor.

That's a harsh joke. Beautiful gentle sweet,
Your wit makes smart things sound dumb: when we look at each other,
Though our eyes see well, the sun's light, dulls our vision: your intellectual ability and beauty is of the same nature as the sunlight Causing wise things to become foolish, and rich to appear poor.

ROSALINE
This proves you wise and rich, for in my eye,--

Well, you must be both wise and rich to say such things, because to me--

BIRON
I am a fool, and full of poverty.

I'm stupid and poor.

ROSALINE
But that you take what doth to you belong,
It were a fault to snatch words from my tongue.

If you would take what belongs to you,
It's a shame you took the words right out of my mouth.

BIRON
O, I am yours, and all that I possess!

O, I am yours completely, please tell me!

ROSALINE
All the fool mine?

All your stupidity is mine?

BIRON
I cannot give you less.

That's all I have.

ROSALINE
Which of the vizards was it that you wore?

Which mask did you wear?

BIRON
Where? when? what vizard? why demand you this?

Where? When? What mask? What are you talking about?

ROSALINE
There, then, that vizard; that superfluous case
That hid the worse and show'd the better face.

There, then, that mask; that pointless mask That hid your ugly face and showed a better one.

FERDINAND
We are described; they'll mock us now

We've been spotted; they'll make fun of us now

downright.

for sure.

DUMAIN

Let us confess and turn it to a jest.

Let's just own up to it and make a joke of it.

PRINCESS

Amazed, my lord? why looks your highness
sad?

Are you surprised, my lord? Why do you look
so sad?

ROSALINE

Help, hold his brows! he'll swoon! Why look
you pale?
Sea-sick, I think, coming from Muscovy.

Help, hold his hair! He'll faint! Why do you look
so pale?
I bet you're sea-sick, if you came from Muscovy.

BIRON

Thus pour the stars down plagues for perjury.
Can any face of brass hold longer out?
Here stand I
lady, dart thy skill at me;
Bruise me with scorn, confound me with a flout;
Thrust thy sharp wit quite through my
ignorance;
Cut me to pieces with thy keen conceit;
And I will wish thee never more to dance,
Nor never more in Russian habit wait.
O, never will I trust to speeches penn'd,
Nor to the motion of a schoolboy's tongue,
Nor never come in vizard to my friend,
Nor woo in rhyme, like a blind harper's song!
Taffeta phrases, silken terms precise,
Three-piled hyperboles, spruce affectation,
Figures pedantical; these summer-flies
Have blown me full of maggot ostentation:
I do forswear them; and I here protest,
By this white glove;--how white the hand, God
knows!--
Henceforth my wooing mind shall be express'd
In russet yeas and honest kersey noes:
And, to begin, wench,--so God help me, la!--
My love to thee is sound, sans crack or flaw.

This is how the universe punishes us for
breaking our oaths Can any bolder personality
hold out any longer? Here I stand
lady, aim your wit at me;
Hurt me with your scorn, destroy me with your
lack of caring; Stab my ignorance with your
sharp wit;
Cut me to pieces with the pride you take in
yourself; And I will never again ask you to
dance, Or ever again be in attendance wearing
Russian clothes. O, never will I trust my own
written words, Nor my immature way of
speaking, Nor ever come in a mask to see my
sweetheart, Nor woo you with poems, like a
blind man's harp song! Phrases like taffeta,
silky terms chosen carefully, Luxurious
hyperboles, tidy behavior and feeling,
Academic figures of speech; these summer-flies
have laid maggot eggs of vulgarity in me:
I give them up; and here I beg,
By this white glove;--how white the hand
underneath, God knows!-- From now on, I will
only speak my mind In simple 'yeses' and honest
plain 'no's And, as a start, woman,--so Gold
help me, law!-- My love to you is unbreakable,
without a crack or a flaw.

ROSALINE

Sans sans, I pray you.

Don't say "without," please.

BIRON

Yet I have a trick
Of the old rage: bear with me, I am sick;
I'll leave it by degrees. Soft, let us see:
Write, 'Lord have mercy on us' on those three;
They are infected; in their hearts it lies;
They have the plague, and caught it of your eyes;
These lords are visited; you are not free,
For the Lord's tokens on you do I see.

PRINCESS
No, they are free that gave these tokens to us.

BIRON
Our states are forfeit: seek not to undo us.

ROSALINE
It is not so; for how can this be true,
That you stand forfeit, being those that sue?

BIRON
Peace! for I will not have to do with you.

ROSALINE
Nor shall not, if I do as I intend.

BIRON
Speak for yourselves; my wit is at an end.

FERDINAND
Teach us, sweet madam, for our rude transgression
Some fair excuse.

PRINCESS
The fairest is confession.
Were not you here but even now disguised?

FERDINAND
Madam, I was.

PRINCESS
And were you well advised?

FERDINAND
I was, fair madam.

*Still I have a trace
of the old fever: bear with me, for I am sick;
but slowly getting better. Softly then, let's see:
Write, 'Lord have mercy on us' on my
companions; They are sick too; they have
sickness in their hearts; They have a plague,
which they caught from your eyes;
These men are infected; you are not free from
blame, Their love-wounds from you are visible.*

*No, the ones who gave us these tokens were free
of infection.*

*We've given up ourselves to you: please don't
destroy that by saying we're 'free.'*

*It's not true; How can it be,
That you are ready to give yourself up, when
you are all prosecutors?*

*Peace, please! For I don't want to have
anything to do with you.*

Neither do I, that's what I intended.

You guys speak now; I've said all I can say.

*Sweet madam, give us, for our crimes
some kind of pardon.*

*Just confess.
Was it you that was here before in a disguise?*

Yes, madam, I was.

And were you in your thinking clearly?

I was, fair madam.

PRINCESS

When you then were here,
What did you whisper in your lady's ear?

When you were here before,
What did you whisper in my ear?

FERDINAND

That more than all the world I did respect her.

That I loved her more than the whole world.

PRINCESS

When she shall challenge this, you will reject
her.

If I were to disbelieve you, you would reject me.

FERDINAND

Upon mine honour, no.

Upon my honor I would not.

PRINCESS

Peace, peace! forbear:
Your oath once broke, you force not to forswear.

Calm, calm! Please refrain:
Once you break a promise, you won't hesitate to
do it again.

FERDINAND

Despise me, when I break this oath of mine.

If I break a promise, you can hate me.

PRINCESS

I will: and therefore keep it. Rosaline,
What did the Russian whisper in your ear?

I will hate you: so keep your promise. Rosaline,
What did the 'Russian' whisper in your ear?

ROSALINE

Madam, he swore that he did hold me dear
As precious eyesight, and did value me
Above this world; adding thereto moreover
That he would wed me, or else die my lover.

Madam, he promised that he loved me
that I was as precious as sight, and that he
valued me above all else in the world; adding
also that he would marry me, or die as my lover.

PRINCESS

God give thee joy of him! the noble lord
Most honourably doth unhold his word.

Well, enjoy him! The noble lord
Will most honorably keep his promise.

FERDINAND

What mean you, madam? by my life, my troth,
I never swore this lady such an oath.

What do you mean by that, madam? By my life,
my truth, I never said that to her.

ROSALINE

By heaven, you did; and to confirm it plain,
You gave me this: but take it, sir, again.

By heaven, yes you did; and I'll prove it,
You have me this: but take it back now, sir.

FERDINAND

My faith and this the princess I did give:

I gave this and my faith to the princess:

118

I knew her by this jewel on her sleeve.

PRINCESS
Pardon me, sir, this jewel did she wear;
And Lord Biron, I thank him, is my dear.
What, will you have me, or your pearl again?

BIRON
Neither of either; I remit both twain.
I see the trick on't: here was a consent,
Knowing aforehand of our merriment,
To dash it like a Christmas comedy:
Some carry-tale, some please-man, some slight zany,
Some mumble-news, some trencher-knight, some Dick,
That smiles his cheek in years and knows the trick
To make my lady laugh when she's disposed,
Told our intents before; which once disclosed,
The ladies did change favours: and then we,
Following the signs, woo'd but the sign of she.
Now, to our perjury to add more terror,
We are again forsworn, in will and error.
Much upon this it is: and might not you

To BOYET
Forestall our sport, to make us thus untrue?
Do not you know my lady's foot by the squier,
And laugh upon the apple of her eye?
And stand between her back, sir, and the fire,
Holding a trencher, jesting merrily?
You put our page out: go, you are allow'd;
Die when you will, a smock shall be your shroud.
You leer upon me, do you? there's an eye
Wounds like a leaden sword.

BOYET
Full merrily
Hath this brave manage, this career, been run.

BIRON
Lo, he is tilting straight! Peace! I have done.

Enter COSTARD

I knew it was her by this jewel on her sleeve.

Pardon me, sir, she did wear that jewel;
And Lord Biron, thankfully, is my love.
What will it be? Would you rather have me or your pearl back?

I don't want either; I refuse both together.
I see the trick you're playing: here you've plotted, Knowing ahead of time of our happiness, Only to destroy it like some Christmas play: You are some story-teller, a bootlicker, a stooge,
a piece of bad news, a parasite, a Schmo, that smiles so hard he wrinkles his cheeks and knows the plot
So you can laugh about it when you're alone, You guessed what we wanted ahead of time, and once you figured it out,
You swapped your garments; and then we, fell for your trap, since we were so moonstruck by the sight of our beloved. Now, to our lies you've added more fear, We are again promised, though each to the wrong woman. It must have happned this way: and couldn't you

have told us what was going on, so we knew the lies? Don't you know how to suit my lady's fancy, And know how to keep her eye amused? And stand between her and the fire, Holding a bowl, and joking around? You betrayed us: Go, you're a fool; Go and die, you can wear a dress since you're always in the company of women. You glare at me, do you? Your eye hurts like a fake sword.

Full and cheerfully
Has this maneuver, this gallop, run its course.

Oh, listen to his comeback! Enough! I'm done with this.

Welcome, pure wit! thou partest a fair fray.

COSTARD
O Lord, sir, they would know
Whether the three Worthies shall come in or no.

BIRON
What, are there but three?

COSTARD
No, sir; but it is vara fine,
For every one pursents three.

BIRON
And three times thrice is nine.

COSTARD
Not so, sir; under correction, sir; I hope it is not so.
You cannot beg us, sir, I can assure you, sir we know
what we know:
I hope, sir, three times thrice, sir,--

BIRON
Is not nine.

COSTARD
Under correction, sir, we know whereuntil it doth amount.

BIRON
By Jove, I always took three threes for nine.

COSTARD
O Lord, sir, it were pity you should get your living
by reckoning, sir.

BIRON
How much is it?

COSTARD
O Lord, sir, the parties themselves, the actors, sir, will show whereuntil it doth amount: for

---

Welcome, witty one! You've interrupted a good fight.

O Lord, they'll know
Whether the three worthy ones shall come in or not.

What, are there only three? There's supposed to be nine.

No, sir; but it is very fine,
because every one of them represents three.

And three times three is nine.

No, sir; If I may correct you, sir; I hope not.
You cannot ask us, sir, I assure you, sir, that we know
what we know:
I hope, sir, that three times three, sir, is---

Is not nine.

If I may, sir, we have know way of knowing what it will amount to.

By God, I've always thought three times three was nine.

O lord, sir, it's a shame that you make a living from your math skills, sir.

How much is three times three then?

O Lord, sir, the people themselves, the actors, Sir, will show what it amounts to: for my

mine
own part, I am, as they say, but to parfect one
man
in one poor man, Pompion the Great, sir.

part, I am, as they say, required to perform a role
of one poor man, Pompion the Great, sir.

BIRON
Art thou one of the Worthies?

Are you one of the Worthy ones?

COSTARD
It pleased them to think me worthy of Pompion
the
Great: for mine own part, I know not the degree
of
the Worthy, but I am to stand for him.

It pleased them to think that I was worthy of the
role of Pompion the
Great: for my own part, I don't know to what
degree of
Worthiness, but I am to play the role.

BIRON
Go, bid them prepare.

Go, tell them to get ready.

COSTARD
We will turn it finely off, sir; we will take
some care.

We will pull it off finely, sir; we will be
careful to do so.

Exit

FERDINAND
Biron, they will shame us: let them not
approach.

Byron they will be a disgrace to us: don't let
them come.

BIRON
We are shame-proof, my lord: and tis some
policy
To have one show worse than the king's and his
company.

We can't be shamed any more than we already
are, my lord: and it's good strategy
To have someone else around more disgraceful
than the king and his company.

FERDINAND
I say they shall not come.

I say they cannot come.

PRINCESS
Nay, my good lord, let me o'errule you now:
That sport best pleases that doth least know
how:
Where zeal strives to content, and the contents
Dies in the zeal of that which it presents:
Their form confounded makes most form in
mirth,
When great things labouring perish in their

No, my good lord, let me overrule your
command: The most fun plays are acted by those
who don't know how to act:
With an enthusiasm to perform, and the
substance of the play Is overshadowed by the
enthusiasm to perform it. Watching them make
a mess of the performance has it's own
pleasure, when great works of art are destroyed

birth.

in their performance.

BIRON
A right description of our sport, my lord.

That's an accurate description of what we do,
my lord.

Enter DON ADRIANO DE ARMADO

DON ADRIANO DE ARMADO
Anointed, I implore so much expense of thy
royal
sweet breath as will utter a brace of words.

Dear anointed one, I ask if you can spare a
moment
To speak with me.

Converses apart with FERDINAND, and delivers him a paper

PRINCESS
Doth this man serve God?

Is this a man of God?

BIRON
Why ask you?

Why do you ask?

PRINCESS
He speaks not like a man of God's making.

He doesn't speak like a man that God made.

DONADRIANO DE ARMADO
That is all one, my fair, sweet, honey monarch;
for,
I protest, the schoolmaster is exceeding
fantastical; too, too vain, too too vain: but we
will put it, as they say, to fortuna de la guerra.
I wish you the peace of mind, most royal
couplement!

That is all the same, my fair, sweet, beautiful
highness; for,
I must disagree, the teacher is far too
fantastical; too, too vain, too too vain: but we
will say, as the saying goes, to the fortune of
war. I wish you peace of mind, most royal
couple!

Exit

FERDINAND
Here is like to be a good presence of Worthies.
He
presents Hector of Troy; the swain, Pompey the
Great; the parish curate, Alexander; Armado's
page,
Hercules; the pedant, Judas Maccabaeus: And if
these four Worthies in their first show thrive,
These four will change habits, and present the
other five.

Here it's like being in the presence of the
Worthy. He
acts like he's Hector of Troy; the country boy
like Pompey the Great; the parish priest like
Alexander; Armado's assistant,
Hercules; the teacher, Judas Maccabaeus: And
if These four Worthy ones in their first show
perform well, They will change their clothes,
and act out the other five roles too.

BIRON
There is five in the first show.

There are five characters in the first play.

FERDINAND
You are deceived; 'tis not so.

You must be deceived; that's not the case.

BIRON
The pedant, the braggart, the hedge-priest, the fool
and the boy:--
Abate throw at novum, and the whole world again
Cannot pick out five such, take each one in his vein.

The teacher, the braggart, the illiterate priest, the fool
And the boy:--
All chance aside, and the whole world couldn't pick out five, they are each such fantastical characters.

FERDINAND
The ship is under sail, and here she comes amain.

It's too late now, here they come.

Enter COSTARD, for Pompey

COSTARD
I Pompey am,--

I am Pompey, --

BOYET
You lie, you are not he.

You lie, you're not Pompey.

COSTARD
I Pompey am,--

I am Pompey,--

BOYET
With libbard's head on knee.

With your coat of arms on your knee rather than your shield.

BIRON
Well said, old mocker: I must needs be friends with thee.

Good one, old heckler: I should be friends with you.

COSTARD
I Pompey am, Pompey surnamed the Big—

I am Pompey, Pompey nicknamed the Big--

DUMAIN
The Great.

The Great.

COSTARD
It is, 'Great,' sir:--
Pompey surnamed the Great;

It is, "Great," sir:--
Pompey nicknamed the Great;

That oft in field, with targe and shield, did make my foe to sweat:
And travelling along this coast, I here am come by chance,
And lay my arms before the legs of this sweet lass of France,
If your ladyship would say, 'Thanks, Pompey,' I had done.

That often in the battlefield, with sword and shield, did make My enemies sweat:
And travelling along the coast, I happen to come here
And lay my shield in front of legs of a sweet girl from France,
If she would only say, 'Thanks, Pompey,' I would be done.

PRINCESS
Great thanks, great Pompey.

Great thanks, great Pompey.

COSTARD
'Tis not so much worth; but I hope I was perfect: I
made a little fault in 'Great.'

It isn't worth much; but I hope I was perfect: I Forgot part of my line.

BIRON
My hat to a halfpenny, Pompey proves the best Worthy.

I tip my hat to you, Pompey seems to be the best Character.

Enter SIR NATHANIEL, for Alexander

SIR NATHANIEL
When in the world I lived, I was the world's commander;
By east, west, north, and south, I spread my conquering might:
My scutcheon plain declares that I am Alisander,--

When I lived in the world, I was the world's commander;
East, west, north, and south, I conquered.
My shield clearly states that I am Alexander,--

BOYET
Your nose says, no, you are not for it stands too right.

Your nose says that you're not, for Alexander's was crooked and yours is straight.

BIRON
Your nose smells 'no' in this, most tender-smelling knight.

You don't think it's him then, you sensitive knight.

PRINCESS
The conqueror is dismay'd. Proceed, good Alexander.

The conqueror has been interrupted. Keep going, Alexander.

SIR NATHANIEL
When in the world I lived, I was the world's

When I lived in the world, I was the world's

124

commander,--

commander,--

BOYET
Most true, 'tis right; you were so, Alisander.

That is most true, 'tis right; you were, Alexander,

BIRON
Pompey the Great,--

Pompey the Great,--

COSTARD
Your servant, and Costard.

At your service, and Costard too.

BIRON
Take away the conqueror, take away Alisander.

Get rid of this conqueror, take away Alexander.

COSTARD
[To SIR NATHANIEL] O, sir, you have overthrown
Alisander the conqueror! You will be scraped out of
the painted cloth for this: your lion, that holds
his poll-axe sitting on a close-stool, will be given
to Ajax: he will be the ninth Worthy. A conqueror,
and afeard to speak! run away for shame, Alisander.

O, sir you have been overthrown Alexander the conqueror! You will be removed from the painting of the characters for this: your lion, holding a battle axe sitting on a toilet, will be given to Ajax: and he will become the ninth Worthy. A conqueror, and you're afraid to speak! Run away in shame, Alexander.

SIR NATHANIEL retires

There, an't shall please you; a foolish mild man; an
honest man, look you, and soon dashed. He is a
marvellous good neighbour, faith, and a very good
bowler: but, for Alisander,--alas, you see how
'tis,--a little o'erparted. But there are Worthies
a-coming will speak their mind in some other sort.

There if it will please you; a foolish and mild man; an Honest man, look if you will, and soon he is destroyed. He is a great neighbor, faithful, and a very good bowler: but, for Alexander,-- well, you see how it is,--the part is a little too difficult for him. But there are other Worthies on their way that will speak better.

Enter HOLOFERNES, for Judas; and MOTH, for Hercules

HOLOFERNES
Great Hercules is presented by this imp,
Whose club kill'd Cerberus, that three-headed canis;
And when he was a babe, a child, a shrimp,

The role of Great Hercules is being acted by this demon child, Whose club killed Cerberus, the three-headed dog; And when he was a baby, a child, a shrimp,

Thus did he strangle serpents in his manus.
Quoniam he seemeth in minority,
Ergo I come with this apology.
Keep some state in thy exit, and vanish.

He strangled snakes with his hands
This is him as a baby,
That's why I come with this apology.
Have some dignity in your exit, and be gone.

MOTH retires

Judas I am,--

I am Judas,--

DUMAIN
A Judas!

A traitor!

HOLOFERNES
Not Iscariot, sir.
Judas I am, ycliped Maccabaeus.

Not Judas Iscariot, the traitor, sir.
I am Judas, called Maccabaeus.

DUMAIN
Judas Maccabaeus clipt is plain Judas.

Judas Maccabaeus is the same as plain Judas.

BIRON
A kissing traitor. How art thou proved Judas?

Judas was a kissing traitor. How do you prove
to be Judas?

HOLOFERNES
Judas I am,--

I am Judas,--

DUMAIN
The more shame for you, Judas.

Too bad for you, Judas.

HOLOFERNES
What mean you, sir?

What do you mean, sir?

BOYET
To make Judas hang himself.

He means to make Judas hang himself.

HOLOFERNES
Begin, sir; you are my elder.

You are my elder, so you should speak first.

BIRON
Well followed: Judas was hanged on an elder.

Good one: Judas was hanged on an elder tree.

HOLOFERNES
I will not be put out of countenance.

I will not break character.

BIRON
Because thou hast no face.

Because you don't have a face.

HOLOFERNES
What is this?

What do you call this? (points to his face)

BOYET
A cittern-head.

A guitar-head.

DUMAIN
The head of a bodkin.

The head of a hairpin.

BIRON
A Death's face in a ring.

A death's head worn on a ring.

LONGAVILLE
The face of an old Roman coin, scarce seen.

The face on some old Roman coin that's been worn smooth.

BOYET
The pommel of Caesar's falchion.

The butt of Caesar's sword.

DUMAIN
The carved-bone face on a flask.

The carved-bone face on a powder horn flask.

BIRON
Saint George's half-cheek in a brooch.

Saint George's profile in a brooch.

DUMAIN
Ay, and in a brooch of lead.

Yeah, and a cheap brooch at that.

BIRON
Ay, and worn in the cap of a tooth-drawer.
And now forward; for we have put thee in
countenance.

Yeah, and a brooch worn in the cap of a lowly dentist. Now keep going; we have to establish your character.

HOLOFERNES
You have put me out of countenance.

You have made me break character.

BIRON
False; we have given thee faces.

False; we have given you many characters.

HOLOFERNES
But you have out-faced them all.

And you have taken the character out of all of them.

BIRON
An thou wert a lion, we would do so.

And if you were a lion, we would do the same.

BOYET
Therefore, as he is an ass, let him go.

Therefore, since he is an ass, let him go on his

And so adieu, sweet Jude! nay, why dost thou stay?

way. And so goodbye, sweet Jude! No, why do you still stand there?

DUMAIN
For the latter end of his name.

He's waiting to hear his last name.

BIRON
For the ass to the Jude; give it him:--Jud-as, away!

For the ass of Jude; give it to him:--Jud-ass, away!

HOLOFERNES
This is not generous, not gentle, not humble.

That is not nice, not gentle, not humble.

BOYET
A light for Monsieur Judas! it grows dark, he may stumble.

Get Master Judas a light! It's getting dark, and he may stumble on his way out.

HOLOFERNES retires

PRINCESS
Alas, poor Maccabaeus, how hath he been baited!

Well, poor Maccabaeus, how he was taunted!

Enter DON ADRIANO DE ARMADO, for Hector

BIRON
Hide thy head, Achilles: here comes Hector in arms.

Watch out, Achilles: here comes Hector with weapons.

DUMAIN
Though my mocks come home by me, I will now be merry.

Though I am mocked, I will now be cheerful.

FERDINAND
Hector was but a Troyan in respect of this.

Hector was just a Trojan in that regard.

BOYET
But is this Hector?

But is that Hector?

FERDINAND
I think Hector was not so clean-timbered.

I didn't think Hector was so well built.

LONGAVILLE
His leg is too big for Hector's.

His leg is too big to be Hector's leg.

DUMAIN
More calf, certain.

A bigger calf, for sure.

BOYET
No; he is best endued in the small.

No; he is best endowed in the ankle.

BIRON
This cannot be Hector.

This cannot be Hector.

DUMAIN
He's a god or a painter; for he makes faces.

He's either a god or a painter; because look at the faces he's making.

DON ADRIANO DE ARMADO
The armipotent Mars, of lances the almighty,
Gave Hector a gift,--

The armed power of Ares, of the almighty lances Gave hector a gift,--

DUMAIN
A gilt nutmeg.

An egg-yolk glazed nutmeg.

BIRON
A lemon.

A lemon.

LONGAVILLE
Stuck with cloves.

A lemon stuck with cloves.

DUMAIN
No, cloven.

No, sliced.

DON ADRIANO DE ARMADO
Peace!—
The armipotent Mars, of lances the almighty
Gave Hector a gift, the heir of Ilion;
A man so breathed, that certain he would fight; yea
From morn till night, out of his pavilion.
I am that flower,--

*Quiet!--
The armed power of Ares, of the almighty lances Gave Hector a gift, the heir of Troy;
A man in such good condition, that he would certainly fight; yes
From morning until night, out of his camp.
I am that flower,--*

DUMAIN
That mint.

That mint.

LONGAVILLE
That columbine.

That columbine flower.

DON ADRIANO DE ARMADO
Sweet Lord Longaville, rein thy tongue.

Sweet Lord Longaville, please control your tongue.

LONGAVILLE
I must rather give it the rein, for it runs against
Hector.

*I'll have to let it go, since it competes against
you.*

DUMAIN
Ay, and Hector's a greyhound.

Yeah, and Hector's fast.

DON ADRIANO DE ARMADO
The sweet war-man is dead and rotten; sweet
chucks,
beat not the bones of the buried: when he
breathed,
he was a man. But I will forward with my
device.

*The sweet warrior is dead and rotten; sweet
chucks,
Don't beat the bones of the buried: when he was
breathing,
he was a man. But I will continue with my
monologue.*

To the PRINCESS
Sweet royalty, bestow on me the sense of
hearing.

*Sweet royalty, please grant me the ability to be
heard.*

PRINCESS
Speak, brave Hector: we are much delighted.

Speak then, brave Hector: we are enjoying this.

DON ADRIANO DE ARMADO
I do adore thy sweet grace's slipper.

I adore your sweet shoe.

BOYET
[Aside to DUMAIN] Loves her by the foot,--

He loves her for her foot,--

DUMAIN
[Aside to BOYET] He may not by the yard.

But not for the yard.

DON ADRIANO DE ARMADO
This Hector far surmounted Hannibal,--

In this Hector was far superior to Hannibal,--

COSTARD
The party is gone, fellow Hector, she is gone;
she
is two months on her way.

*Jaquenetta is gone, Hector, she is gone; she
has been gone for two months.*

DON ADRIANO DE ARMADO
What meanest thou?

What do you mean?

COSTARD
Faith, unless you play the honest Troyan, the
poor

*Have faith, unless you play the honest Trojan,
the poor*

wench is cast away: she's quick; the child brags in
her belly already: tis yours.

*woman has been cast out: she's pregnant; the unborn child brags in
her womb already: It's your child.*

DON ADRIANO DE ARMADO
Dost thou infamonize me among potentates? thou shalt die.

Do you slander me among statesmen? You will die.

COSTARD
Then shall Hector be whipped for Jaquenetta that is
quick by him and hanged for Pompey that is dead by

*Then Hector will be whipped in Jaquenetta's place since she is made
pregnant by him and hanged for killing Pompey.*

DUMAIN
Most rare Pompey!

What a unique Pompey!

BOYET
Renowned Pompey!

The best Pompey!

BIRON
Greater than great, great, great, great Pompey! Pompey the Huge!

Greater than great, great, great, great Pompey! Pompey the Huge!

DUMAIN
Hector trembles.

Look at Hector trembling.

BIRON
Pompey is moved. More Ates, more Ates! stir them
on! stir them on!

*Pompey is moved emotionally. More mischief, more mischief! Stir them!
Stir them!*

DUMAIN
Hector will challenge him.

Hector's going to challenge him.

BIRON
Ay, if a' have no man's blood in's belly than will sup a flea.

Yeah, if he's enough of a man to feed a flea.

DON ADRIANO DE ARMADO
By the north pole, I do challenge thee.

By the north pole, I challenge you to a duel.

COSTARD
I will not fight with a pole, like a northern man: I'll slash; I'll do it by the sword. I bepray you, let me borrow my arms again.

I will not fight with a pole, like a ruffian: I'll slash at you; I'll do it with a sword. I promise you, Let me find my weapons again.

DUMAIN
Room for the incensed Worthies!

Make room for the angry characters!

COSTARD
I'll do it in my shirt.

I'll strip down to my shirt.

DUMAIN
Most resolute Pompey!

Pompey is so decisive!

MOTH
Master, let me take you a buttonhole lower. Do you
not see Pompey is uncasing for the combat? What mean
you? You will lose your reputation.

*Master, let me undress you a bit more. Don't
you
see Pompey is undressing for battle? What do
you mean?
He will humiliate you.*

DON ADRIANO DE ARMADO
Gentlemen and soldiers, pardon me; I will not combat
in my shirt.

*Gentlemen and soldiers, forgive me; I will not
battle
In my shirt.*

DUMAIN
You may not deny it: Pompey hath made the challenge.

*You can't refuse: Pompey accepted your
challenge.*

DON ADRIANO DE ARMADO
Sweet bloods, I both may and will.

Sweet brothers, I can and I will.

BIRON
What reason have you for't?

What's your reason for denying the challenge?

DON ADRIANO DE ARMADO
The naked truth of it is, I have no shirt; I go
woolward for penance.

*The truth is, I'm not wearing any underwear; I
let the wool punish my flesh as a penance.*

BOYET
True, and it was enjoined him in Rome for want of
linen: since when, I'll be sworn, he wore none but
a dishclout of Jaquenetta's, and that a' wears next
his heart for a favour.

*True, and when Hector was challenged in Rome
he had a lack of
underwear: when, I swear, he wore nothing but
a dishcloth of Jaquenetta's and that he wore
next to
his heart as a charm.*

Enter MERCADE

MERCADE
God save you, madam!

God save you, madam!

PRINCESS
Welcome, Mercade;
But that thou interrupt'st our merriment.

Welcome in, Mercade;
But you're interrupting our enjoyment.

MERCADE
I am sorry, madam; for the news I bring
Is heavy in my tongue. The king your father--

I am sorry, madam; but the news I have
is hard to say. The king your father--

PRINCESS
Dead, for my life!

Is he dead? Oh my life!

MERCADE
Even so; my tale is told.

I'm afraid so; now you know.

BIRON
Worthies, away! the scene begins to cloud.

Actors, get out of here! This is not a good time.

DON ADRIANO DE ARMADO
For mine own part, I breathe free breath. I have
seen the day of wrong through the little hole of
discretion, and I will right myself like a soldier.

For myself, I am a free man. I now
Perceive my true situation
and will carry on like a trooper.

Exeunt Worthies

FERDINAND
How fares your majesty?

How are you doing princess?

PRINCESS
Boyet, prepare; I will away tonight.

Prepare yourself, Boyet; I need to leave tonight.

FERDINAND
Madam, not so; I do beseech you, stay.

Madam, you do not; I beg of you, please stay.

PRINCESS
Prepare, I say. I thank you, gracious lords,
For all your fair endeavors; and entreat,
Out of a new-sad soul, that you vouchsafe
In your rich wisdom to excuse or hide
The liberal opposition of our spirits,
If over-boldly we have borne ourselves
In the converse of breath: your gentleness
Was guilty of it. Farewell worthy lord!
A heavy heart bears not a nimble tongue:

Get ready, I say. Thank you, gracious lords,
For all the fun; and allow me
With my broken heart, that you promise
In your wisdom to let me be excused or overlook
Our disagreeing,
If we have portrayed ourselves too boldly
In our conversation: you
were guilty too. Farewell worthy lord!
A heavy heart can't stand a quick talker:

Excuse me so, coming too short of thanks
For my great suit so easily obtain'd.

Excuse me, for being so ungrateful
but my mission was already accomplished.

FERDINAND

The extreme parts of time extremely forms
All causes to the purpose of his speed,
And often at his very loose decides
That which long process could not arbitrate:
And though the mourning brow of progeny
Forbid the smiling courtesy of love
The holy suit which fain it would convince,
Yet, since love's argument was first on foot,
Let not the cloud of sorrow justle it
From what it purposed; since, to wail friends lost
Is not by much so wholesome-profitable
As to rejoice at friends but newly found.

When time is short, it
requires quick decisions,
And often at time's very release a decision is
reached That if I had thought about it a long
time I would not be able to decide: And though
the princess is in mourning And will not see my
love's argument And the love which I would like
to give her, Yet, since the argument was running
first, Don't allow sorrow to obstruct it
From what it wanted; since, to cry about lost
friends
is not good for anything
as it is to rejoice at making new friends.

PRINCESS

I understand you not: my griefs are double.

I don't understand you: that doubles my grief.

BIRON

Honest plain words best pierce the ear of grief;
And by these badges understand the king.
For your fair sakes have we neglected time,
Play'd foul play with our oaths: your beauty, ladies,
Hath much deform'd us, fashioning our humours
Even to the opposed end of our intents:
And what in us hath seem'd ridiculous,--
As love is full of unbefitting strains,
All wanton as a child, skipping and vain,
Form'd by the eye and therefore, like the eye,
Full of strange shapes, of habits and of forms,
Varying in subjects as the eye doth roll
To every varied object in his glance:
Which parti-coated presence of loose love
Put on by us, if, in your heavenly eyes,
Have misbecomed our oaths and gravities,
Those heavenly eyes, that look into these faults,
Suggested us to make. Therefore, ladies,
Our love being yours, the error that love makes
Is likewise yours: we to ourselves prove false,
By being once false for ever to be true
To those that make us both,--fair ladies, you:

If you want to reach her through her grief use
simple words when you do so she will
understand you. For your sake, we have
forgotten about time, and nearly broke our
promises: your beauty, ladies
Has greatly deformed us, making our moods
Opposite from what we intended:
And what to us seemed ridiculous,--
as love gives you strange impulses,
As carefree as a child, skipping and vain,
Formed by the eye and therefore, like the eye
It is full of strange shapes, habits and forms,
From one thing to the other as the eye rolls
To every object the eye can see:
With the foolish appearance that love
gives us, if, in your heavenly eyes,
We have become unsuitable for our promises
and positions, Your heavenly eyes, that see these
mistakes tempted us to make. Therefore, ladies,
Since our love is yours, the mistakes love makes
is also yours: we prove ourselves false,
If we are false once we will forever be true
to those that make us both false and true,-- fair

And even that falsehood, in itself a sin,
Thus purifies itself and turns to grace.

PRINCESS
We have received your letters full of love;
Your favours, the ambassadors of love;
And, in our maiden council, rated them
At courtship, pleasant jest and courtesy,
As bombast and as lining to the time:
But more devout than this in our respects
Have we not been; and therefore met your loves
In their own fashion, like a merriment.

DUMAIN
Our letters, madam, show'd much more than
jest.

LONGAVILLE
So did our looks.

ROSALINE
We did not quote them so.

FERDINAND
Now, at the latest minute of the hour,
Grant us your loves.

PRINCESS
A time, methinks, too short
To make a world-without-end bargain in.
No, no, my lord, your grace is perjured much,
Full of dear guiltiness; and therefore this:
If for my love, as there is no such cause,
You will do aught, this shall you do for me:
Your oath I will not trust; but go with speed
To some forlorn and naked hermitage,
Remote from all the pleasures of the world;
There stay until the twelve celestial signs
Have brought about the annual reckoning.
If this austere insociable life
Change not your offer made in heat of blood;
If frosts and fasts, hard lodging and thin weeds
Nip not the gaudy blossoms of your love,
But that it bear this trial and last love;
Then, at the expiration of the year,
Come challenge me, challenge me by these

*ladies, that means you: And even that falsehood,
which is in itself a sin, will purify itself and turn
in to grace.*

*We have received your love letters;
Your tokens, the symbols of love;
And, when we spoke about it privately, decided
it Was only dating, pleasant jokes and manners
As a way to fill time,
But serious in this respect
we have not been; and for this reason saw your
loves In that way, as a joke or a pleasant way to
pass time.*

*Our letters, madam, were more than just joking
around.*

And our looks were serious as well.

That's not how we perceived it.

*Now, before we are out of time,
Give us your loves.*

*I think there's not enough time
To make that kind of everlasting bargain.
No, no, my lord, your grace has been betrayed,
you are full of guilt; and therefore I say this:
If you would, for my love, as there is nothing
like it, do anything, then do this for me:
I can't trust your promise; but go quickly
to some lonely and barren hermitage,
Far away from all the modern pleasures of the
world; And stay there until twelve months
Have gone buy to mark one year.
If this severe nonsocial life
won't change the offer you made in passion;
If frost and hunger, rough shelter and thin
garments Don't degrade the intensity of your
love, But if you can bear this trial and love
remains; Then, after one year
Come claim me, claim me by the merit of these*

deserts,
And, by this virgin palm now kissing thine
I will be thine; and till that instant shut
My woeful self up in a mourning house,
Raining the tears of lamentation
For the remembrance of my father's death.
If this thou do deny, let our hands part,
Neither entitled in the other's heart.

actions,
And, by my virgin hand, which you are now
kissing I will be yours; and until a year has
passed I will shut my woeful self up in my house
to mourn, Raining tears in lament
Over my father's death.
If you won't do this, then let us not touch,
Neither of us has a right to the other.

FERDINAND
If this, or more than this, I would deny,
To flatter up these powers of mine with rest,
The sudden hand of death close up mine eye!
Hence ever then my heart is in thy breast.

If this request, or more than this request, I
would refuse And instead pamper up myself with
rest, Then the hand of death will take me!
So my heart will forever be in your chest.

DUMAIN
But what to me, my love? but what to me? A
wife?

What do I get, my love? What do I get? A wife?

KATHARINE
A beard, fair health, and honesty;
With three-fold love I wish you all these three.

A beard, good health, and honesty;
With all my love I wish for you to have these
three things.

DUMAIN
O, shall I say, I thank you, gentle wife?

O, should I say, I thank you, wife?

KATHARINE
Not so, my lord; a twelvemonth and a day
I'll mark no words that smooth-faced wooers
say:
Come when the king doth to my lady come;
Then, if I have much love, I'll give you some.

No, my lord; not fore twelve months and a day
I won't listen to any words beardless suitors say
Come to me when the king comes to the
princess;
Then, if I feel like it, I'll love you.

DUMAIN
I'll serve thee true and faithfully till then.

I'll wait for you true and faithfully until then.

KATHARINE
Yet swear not, lest ye be forsworn again.

Don't swear it, unless you break another
promise.

LONGAVILLE
What says Maria?

What do you say Maria?

MARIA
At the twelvemonth's end
I'll change my black gown for a faithful friend.

At the end of twelve months
I'll take of my black dress for a faithful lover.

LONGAVILLE
I'll stay with patience; but the time is long.

I'll remain with patience; but it is such a long time.

MARIA
The liker you; few taller are so young.

Just like you; there are few young people who are so tall.

BIRON
Studies my lady? mistress, look on me;
Behold the window of my heart, mine eye,
What humble suit attends thy answer there:
Impose some service on me for thy love.

What are you thinking my lady? Mistress, look at me; See the window of my heart, my eye What humble offering awaits your answer there: Let me do something to earn your love.

ROSALINE
Oft have I heard of you, my Lord Biron,
Before I saw you; and the world's large tongue
Proclaims you for a man replete with mocks,
Full of comparisons and wounding flouts,
Which you on all estates will execute
That lie within the mercy of your wit.
To weed this wormwood from your fruitful brain,
And therewithal to win me, if you please,
Without the which I am not to be won,
You shall this twelvemonth term from day to day
Visit the speechless sick and still converse
With groaning wretches; and your task shall be,
With all the fierce endeavor of your wit
To enforce the pained impotent to smile.

I've heard quite a bit about you, my Lord Biron, before I saw you; and the general consensus claims you to be a man who mocks others, Full of witty sarcastic similes and harsh disregard, Which you would place on all classes that you were able to insult.
To get this poison from your intelligent brain, And in doing so, win me, if you'd like to, But without that you'll never win me During this twelve month term, every day, you will
Visit those that are too ill to speak and still have a conversation with groaning sick people; and your task will be, with all the ability of your wit to cause these poor sick people to smile.

BIRON
To move wild laughter in the throat of death?
It cannot be; it is impossible:
Mirth cannot move a soul in agony.

To cause dying people to laugh? It can't be; it's impossible: Jokes cannot cause an agonized soul to feel happy.

ROSALINE
Why, that's the way to choke a gibing spirit,
Whose influence is begot of that loose grace
Which shallow laughing hearers give to fools:
A jest's prosperity lies in the ear
Of him that hears it, never in the tongue
Of him that makes it: then, if sickly ears,
Deaf'd with the clamours of their own dear groans,
Will hear your idle scorns, continue then,
And I will have you and that fault withal;

Well, that's the only way to stop a mocking spirit, whose influence gets too much approval by people laughing shallowly at your foolish jokes: A joke's value lies in the way it's heard by him that hears it, rather than the way it's told by the one who speaks it: then, if it's heard by the sick Deafened with the sound of their own groans, will hear your dumb insults, then keep making them, and I will accept you and all of your

But if they will not, throw away that spirit,
And I shall find you empty of that fault,
Right joyful of your reformation.

faults; But if they don't, stop your habit of mocking, and I will find you free of flaws, And happy to see you've changed.

BIRON
A twelvemonth! well; befall what will befall,
I'll jest a twelvemonth in an hospital.

Twelve months! Well; let happen what will happen, I'll joke for twelve months in a hospital

PRINCESS
[To FERDINAND] Ay, sweet my lord; and so I take my leave.

Ok, my sweet lord; I will leave now.

FERDINAND
No, madam; we will bring you on your way.

No, madam; let us go with you a ways.

BIRON
Our wooing doth not end like an old play;
Jack hath not Jill: these ladies' courtesy
Might well have made our sport a comedy.

Our attempts to win them over didn't have a storybook ending Jack did not win Jill: these ladies' manners might have made our attempts a joke.

FERDINAND
Come, sir, it wants a twelvemonth and a day,
And then 'twill end.

Come on, sir, we have to wait twelve months and a day, And then our play will end.

BIRON
That's too long for a play.

That's too long for a play.

Re-enter DON ADRIANO DE ARMADO

DON ADRIANO DE ARMADO
Sweet majesty, vouchsafe me,--

Sweet majesty, grant me,--

PRINCESS
Was not that Hector?

Isn't that Hector?

DUMAIN
The worthy knight of Troy.

Hector, the worthy knight of Troy.

DON ADRIANO DE ARMADO
I will kiss thy royal finger, and take leave. I am
a votary; I have vowed to Jaquenetta to hold the
plough for her sweet love three years. But, most
esteemed greatness, will you hear the dialogue
that
the two learned men have compiled in praise of

I will kiss your royal finger, and leave. I have made a religious vow; I have vowed to Jaquenetta to work with a plough to win her sweet love for three years. But, most honorable king, will you hear that dialogue that the two educated men came up with in praise of

the
owl and the cuckoo? It should have followed in
the
end of our show.

the
owl and the cuckoo? It was supposed to be at
the
end of our show.

FERDINAND
Call them forth quickly; we will do so.

Tell them to come quickly; we will hear it.

DON ADRIANO DE ARMADO
Holla! approach.

Hey! Approach the stage.

Re-enter HOLOFERNES, SIR NATHANIEL, MOTH, COSTARD, and others

This side is Hiems, Winter, this Ver, the Spring;
the one maintained by the owl, the other by the
cuckoo. Ver, begin.

This character is Hiems, portraying winter, and
this is Ver, portraying Spring; The winter is
played by the owl, the other is played by the
Cuckoo. Ver, begin.

THE SONG

SPRING.
When daisies pied and violets blue
And lady-smocks all silver-white
And cuckoo-buds of yellow hue
Do paint the meadows with delight,
The cuckoo then, on every tree,
Mocks married men; for thus sings he, Cuckoo;
Cuckoo, cuckoo: O word of fear,
Unpleasing to a married ear!
When shepherds pipe on oaten straws
And merry larks are ploughmen's clocks,
When turtles tread, and rooks, and daws,
And maidens bleach their summer smocks
The cuckoo then, on every tree,
Mocks married men; for thus sings he, Cuckoo;
Cuckoo, cuckoo: O word of fear,
Unpleasing to a married ear!

When multicolored daisies and blue violets
And silver-white lady's smocks
And cuckoo-blossoms of a yellow hue
Paint the meadows with delightful colors,
The cuckoo will then sit on every tree,
and Mock married men; for he sings like this,
Cuckoo; Cuckoo, cuckoo: O the scary word
So unpleasant to someone who is married!
When shepherds chew on weeds
And happy larks serve as clocks to the field
workers, when turtles walk, and crows and jack-
daws, And maidens wash their summer dresses
The cuckoo will then sit on every tree,
and mock married men; for he sings like this,
Cuckoo; Cuckoo, cuckoo: O scary word
So unpleasant to someone who is married!

WINTER.
When icicles hang by the wall
And Dick the shepherd blows his nail
And Tom bears logs into the hall
And milk comes frozen home in pail,
When blood is nipp'd and ways be foul,
Then nightly sings the staring owl, Tu-whit;
Tu-who, a merry note,
While greasy Joan doth keel the pot.

When icicles have formed by the wall
And Dick the shepherd blows on his hands to
keep them warm And Tom brings logs into the
hall And milk is frozen in the pail by the time
you bring it home When blood is cold and
moods are foul, Then every night will sing the
staring owl, Tu-whit; Tu-who, a happy song,
While greasy Joan keeps stirring the pot.

When all aloud the wind doth blow
And coughing drowns the parson's saw
And birds sit brooding in the snow
And Marian's nose looks red and raw,
When roasted crabs hiss in the bowl,
Then nightly sings the staring owl, Tu-whit;
Tu-who, a merry note,
While greasy Joan doth keel the pot.

When the wind blows loudly
And winter coughs drown the parson's snoring
And birds sit unmoving in the snow
And Marian's nose appears red and raw,
When roasted crabs hiss in the bowl,
Then every night the staring owl will sing, Tu-whit; Tu-who, a happy song,
While greasy Joan keeps stirring the pot.

DON ADRIANO DE ARMADO
The words of Mercury are harsh after the songs of
Apollo. You that way: we this way.

The words of Hermes, god of eloquence, are harsh after the song of
Apollo, god of music: You go that way: we will go this way.

Exeunt

Printed in Great Britain
by Amazon

38802548R00079